ALIENS
BELIEVE TOO!
Written by
Brian Hiller

Illustration Information:

 The front and rear cover art conception was
originally created and drafted by the Author, Brian
Hiller. His idea was to perceive the likeness of a
movie poster. On the rear cover, he thought of a
different approach for his photo, by the use of CG
animation.

 Later, he met with Artist Marianne Bell...she
identifying with Brian's vision to achieve a new and
unique final art illustration. Marianne performed the
final illustration work with oil and acrylic based
paints, to display a more realistic and three
dimensional looking scenery. Brian greatly
acknowledges Marianne's inspiring, and fascinating
talent for Art.

To My Family and Friends:

Love and thanks to my son Brian Jr., Mother,
Father, Grandfathers, Grandmothers, Brother
Bobby, Sisters Patty, Kitty, Evie, Aunts, Uncles,
Nephews, Nieces, Tamarita and Kids, Jim and
Debbie, Marianne, Janet Lee, Dana, David,
Mary, Barbara, and Everyone who's been a true
Friend and supportive to me through the years.
Special Thanks:
Theresa Hiller, Tamarita and Kids, Marianne
Bell, Robert F., Nan, Lulu Publishing,
Lisa and Jim, and once again my loving Mom.

Introduction

Outer space…what locked secrets does it hold in its depths? The many unanswered questions from the past to present, in mankind's will and devotion to discover all of its mysteries?
Perhaps the biggest question of all…are, or are we not alone in the Universe?

With all of the endless strange and bizarre accounts of UFO sightings, and alien abductions, we are only to wonder…what could be extra terrestrial's motives, and why Earth? Without any real concrete evidence...we shall continue to believe in the possibility of other life forms existing in our great Universe.

Brian Hiller

ALIENS
BELIEVE TOO!

Table of Contents:

CHAPTER 1
VISITATION

The time is about seven thirty pm. and very dark
in a backyard somewhere in Arizona, as a young
man in his late thirties, James Lowery, Caucasian,
dressed in slacks, a loosely buttoned shirt, holding a
full glass of wine and crouched over a telescope
views the clear starlit heavens. Suddenly what
resembles a slow shooting star, streaks across the
sky. "Well hello there," says James as he tracks its
course intently. The so-called shooting star
suddenly stops briefly, then descends out of sight.
"What the hell," says James as he quickly raises
his head with a look of amazement at the dark
desert horizon. He then grabs the front of the
telescope and spins it around for an observation of
any debris on the lens. The lens appearing spotless,
he looks at the horizon again, then his glass of wine.
"Good stuff." He downs the entire drink then
exhales, "Ahhhh." Suddenly a young woman's glistening
voice from behind James asks, "Any signs of life yet?"
James instantly wears a grin as he turns around to reply,
"As a matter of fact." He then walks up to a beautiful
young woman, his wife Debbie,
Caucasian, blonde, green eyes, curvy, dressed in a
sheer nightgown, and holding a glass of wine. They
softly embrace each other and James continues,
"My little green friends were thinking about coming over
for dinner tonight." Debbie smiles while saying, "In that
case, I'll see what I can whip up." With no delay, they kiss
passionately. James sets his glass down on the edge of a
table, but it falls to the ground and shatters. He then swoops
Debbie up into his arms. She moans a little as they continue
kissing. James then carries her into the house via the
French doors. Meanwhile, viewing the dark horizon,

James and Debbie's moans, and the sound of Debbie's wine glass shattering on the floor are heard, as a brief flicker of blue light appears on the horizon.

Located at the base of several desert hills in the moonlit night, exists a ranch with your traditional red barn, an old pickup, various animals, and a mobile home adorned with wooden plaques and wind brushed wind chimes singing their own melody. The front door of the mobile home suddenly swings open, and an old man, Jessie Taylor, Caucasian, gray hair and beard, wearing overalls and a straw cowboy hat steps outside. An old woman's voice, Jessie's wife Kate, blares over the sound of the television, "And don't furget to feed Lila!"
"Yeah yeah yeah," Jessie replies as he slams the door and walks away toward the barn. He strolls up to the right front side of the barn, picks up an old bucket, and begins to fill it with oats from a dispenser located on the corner of the barn. In the pitch-black barn, several horses in stalls begin to act spooked, and begin to buck and kick. Jessie still filling up the bucket shouts, "Oh quit your whining! I'm a feedin yeas!" The rest of the animals also begin to act restless as Jessie finishes filling the bucket, and walks up to the front entrance of the barn. Gust's of wind suddenly begin blowing all around. The sound of wood breaking, and the horse's yowling as Jessie is almost trampled by the horses running out of the barn. He quickly steps back and shouts at them, "Git back here! Ya durn blasted no good varmints!"

9

The horses continue to run away, as a bright blue light
shines from behind on Jessie. His eyes widen
and roll side to side as he slowly turns around
towards it. Once fully turned, his eyes widen even
more as his jaw drops along with the bucket of oats.
The light intensifies, as a swift wind removes
Jessie's hat. A moment later, the front door of the
mobile opens and Kate, Caucasian, wearing a dress
with an apron steps out and shouts, "Jessie?"
Suddenly the bright blue light shines down on her.
She looks up and screams with a deafening shriek.

   The light of day now shines through the curtains
of James and Debbie's room, as James lay half naked, and
half covered with a sheet, hugging a
pillow. A clock radio time reads seven thirty am.
The minutes suddenly flip over to eight o'clock in a
matter of seconds. The radio comes on playing
rock'n roll, then James rolls over still hugging the
pillow, and starts kissing it. "Oh baby," James softly
moans. He suddenly realizes his foolishness, opens his eyes
and tosses the pillow away. He sits up and yawns aloud and
long, then smacks the top of the clock radio, shutting it off.
He grabs a television remote, points it at his television
located at the foot of his bed and clicks it on. He then leans
back on the
headboard. On the television, a news anchor, Bob
Spencer, Caucasian, in his early fifties doing the
morning news, "Good morning, and welcome back to the
eight o'clock report. And now with a further update on the
strange sightings of lights that have been
reoccurring for the past month, I turn your attention
to my colleague Debbie Lowery."

Debbie appears brisk and gleaming. "Hello beautiful," says James in an introductory voice. "Thank you Bob. Yes, that's right folks. The strange unidentified lights in the night skies are at it again. Several people have reported sightings of the lights at all hours of the night last night. We spoke with local police and government officials about the sightings, but neither of them could give an explanation as to what they are, or where they come from." Debbie turns to Bob. "What do you think Bob? Possibly UFOs? Or someone playing a practical joke?" Debbie smiles and lifts a cup of coffee to sip. Bob replies, "Well, you know what they say Debbie? Seeing is believing." James lifts the television remote and clicks off the television. "A believer, you're not." He then jumps out of bed with the sheet around him, and walks toward his master bathroom. His cell phone on the dresser rings with a cosmic tone. He answers it. "Hello, the one and only James Lowery speaking. How might I be of service to you?" An older man's raspy voice on the phone...
"You can start by setting your alarm clock. It's past eight Lowery."
"Oh, hello sir. Sorry! It won't happen again."
"I'll let it slide, on account of it's your Anniversary."
"Thank you Sir."
"Yeah. Now get your ass down here!"
"Right away sir."
James hangs up and begins mocking the man's voice on the phone, as he walks to the bathroom. "It's past eight Lowery. I'll let it slide. Now get your ass down here."

In an elevator, James stands alone wearing a brown leather sport jacket, blue jeans and dress

shirt, with snake skin boots as he grooms his hair.
The elevator doors open and James steps out.
Dozens of people, working in dozens of cubicles,
mulling around. A coworker, Todd Barker,
Caucasian, late twenties and a little on the heavy
side, approaches James. "Hey look everyone!
Lowery's just in time for lunch!" Everyone looks
briefly, as James crosses his arms and sighs. "What
is it this time Barker... lose your bone?"
"Ha ha. Just wanted to wish you a Happy Second
Lowery."
"I'm touched. You really mean that?"
"Not," replies Todd with a smile.
Todd turns and takes a few steps, then turns to
James again. "Oh by the way, I see your wife's
more on top of things these days."
Todd turns and walks away, as James smiles and
pats his chest briefly.
"Ho ho ho! You're so funny Barker. Next time I'll
equip myself with an extra pair of underwear just
for you!" James quickly points toward Todd
briefly. The man from James' phone call, his boss
Dan Olsen, Caucasian, half-bald and gray with a
beer gut stands in an office doorway and shouts,
"Lowery!" James smiles and walks towards him.
"Coming Sir." They both enter the office, the walls lined
with awards, trophies, etc…and Olsen sits in his chair
behind a large mahogany desk, James stands.
"Shut the door and have a seat Lowery." James
closes the door, then takes a seat in front of Olsen.
Olsen lights a cigar and opens the conversation.
"I'm under the assumption you've seen the news
this morning?"
"Just a glimpse."

"A glimpse of the ongoing decline of this paper."
"How do you mean Sir?"
"Never mind. What's more important…is that we get the ball rolling again. Like this strange light stuff going on. As stupid as it sounds, that stories getting a lot of attention…and more attention means what Lowery?"
"More publicity?"
"No Lowery. More papers sold."
"Right, right."
"Lowery?"
"Yes Sir?"
"This paper was here, long before radio or television was even invented! You know that?"
"True Sir?"
"Which brings us to a solution."
"A solution sir?"
"Yes."
Olsen stands up, walks around to the front of the desk and sits in front of James. Olsen continues, "You're gonna get your rear end out there, and get to the bottom, or top of this deal with those lights. This time you're going to do it my way, and my rules. You've cost this paper way too much in the past! Understand me?"
"Completely."
"Good. There's one more thing."
"What's that Sir?"
"I don't want, and don't care to here about any of your theories of aliens, or any other shit like it. Facts Lowery. Capiche?"
"Well Sir." Olsen quickly points his finger at James. "I'm warning you Lowery! Don't even think about it!"

James mimics a hand drill on his head briefly, then replies, "Nothing. Clean as a whistle." James briefly whistles. Olsen returns to his seat.
"Amusing. Now get out of here, and bring me something back I can print on the front page, to crank things up." James nods and stands up, then walks to the door, opens it and looks at Olsen.
"I'll try, not to let you down Sir."
"You'd better not, for your own sake."
"Right Sir."
James briefly waves with half a smile and exits the office, shutting the door hard at the last second. James looks at everyone watching, as Olsen shouts his name. James smiles and adjusts his shirt collar, then walks away while whistling.

CHAPTER 2
OBSERVATION

Inside the local police department, a
policewoman, Dixie, black, forties, sitting at the
dispatch desk takes a call. "Hello, police
department. How may I help you sir?" A brief
moment. "Did you say the Taylor Ranch sir. OK. Thank
you very much sir." She hangs up, then gets up and walks
over to a door that reads: Chief Miles Davis. She knocks. A
man's voice replies, "YES!"
She opens the door and enters. Once inside, she
approaches a black man in uniform, Chief Miles
Davis, mid-forties, sitting back in his chair,
spinning the wheels on a toy police car.
"Sir, a man just reported horses roaming loose
near the Taylor Ranch." Davis puts the toy car down and
replies, "That's twice this month now."
He stands up and puts on his hat while saying, "I'll
go myself this time and check it out."

   In front of the Chronicle James walks out and
approaches his white mini-van. He presses his unlock
button on his key chain. Suddenly two men, appearing to be
Caucasian, mid aged, wearing plain clothes, and dark
shades approach James. James goes to open his door when
one of the men asks, "Mr. Lowery?" James turns to them
and replies, "Yes, who are you gentleman?"
"Who we are is of no importance. But as a matter
of National Security, it is."
"Let me guess? Was it something I said, or wrote
about in my columns?"
"No Sir. It's of another nature."
"Like what?"
"Mr. Lowery, we know of your past surveillance
schemes near our facilities. And we're here to

inform you, that we'll be watching your every
move." James smiles and replies, "Oh no, you guys have
mistaken me for someone else. I can assure you of that."
"Never the less Mr. Lowery. We'll be watching.
Have a good day." The men turn and walk away.
James says aloud, "You too!" Then under his
breath "Moron's," as he opens his door and gets in
his van. He starts it up, revs the engine, then throws
it in gear peeling away... Smoke everywhere.

   On a dirt road just out of town, Davis is driving
his squad car. On the side of the road some seventy
yards ahead of him, a horse stands alone eating
grass. Davis slows down and pulls up near the
horse, keeping a safe distance so not to frighten it.
He shuts the car off and exits ever so calmly. He
slowly walks over to the horse.
"Easy boy." The horse looks at him, as he
continues to approach it. "No one's gonna hurt ya."
Davis stops just a foot away, and gently pets the
horse's forehead. "That a boy."

   At the Taylor Ranch, the front gates are wide open
as Davis walks up with the horse led by a leash he
fabricated from his T-shirt. He leads the horse in
through the gates, and removes the leash. The horse
trots away as Davis walks up to the mobile home.
The front door of the mobile still wide open, as
Davis draws his gun. "Jessie? Kate?" He shouts aloud.
With no reply, Davis continues to approach the
mobile home. He cautiously looks all around,
seeing the old pickup and the spilled bucket of oats
in front of the barn. He reaches the entrance of the

mobile home and says aloud, "Hello? Anyone in there?" Still no reply, he enters. Inside he looks around a little, and then steps back outside and holsters his gun. He uses his shoulder radio. "Nelson?" A man's voice, Nelson's, replies. "Yes sir?"
"I want you and Barnes to come out and meet me here at the Taylor's ranch."
"We're both eating lunch right now sir. We can be there." Davis interrupts,
"Now Nelson!"
"Right away sir."
"And bring a horse trailer."
"Did you say a horse trailer?"
"Yes! A horse trailer Nelson!"
"Understood sir."
Davis takes off his hat and wipes the sweat away from his forehead. "What in the world could have happened here?" He looks in wonder all around.

   In front of the local television news station, James' van pulls in and parks. He steps out and shuts the door, but the engine suffers pre-ignition knock briefly, stopping with a loud backfire. James imitates a gun with his finger pointed at the van, then blows on his finger and pretends to holster it, as he walks towards the station entrance.
Inside the news station, James walks down a hallway past several personnel, finally stopping at a door that reads: News Anchor Debbie Lowery.
He knocks with a ratter tat tat. "Who's there" Debbie asks out loud. James comically replies, "Just your average secret admire!" Inside Debbie stands by the door with a smile. "A secret admire? My husband

would be insanely jealous if he heard about this!"
"I'm willing to keep a secret, if you are?"
"I guess it's all right." Debbie opens the door and James
wraps his arms around her and kisses her as he pulls her
into the office, then kicks the door shut with his foot. They
kiss until they both run out of breath, and gasp in each
other's face. "Not, now James."
"Just five baby?" Debbie nod's, "Ok, just five."
They kiss passionately again and fall backwards out
of view with a thud noise. "Ow!" James shouts.

  Back at the Taylor ranch, Davis watching a
marked suburban backing a horse trailer up to the
barn opening. It stops and two policeman, both
Caucasian, Randy Nelson, thirties, and Jeff Barnes,
late twenties, exit the vehicle and walk to the back
of the trailer. They lower the trailer ramp and two
horses walk out into the barn. "Whelp, that's the
last of them," says Nelson. Davis walks up to the
trailer, takes off his hat and leans on the trailer.
"I need not remind you men of the circumstances
we'll face if this gets out to the media. So I expect
you two to keep this under wraps. That is until we
find out what happened."
"We understand Chief," says Nelson.
"Good! You boys can go now. I'll catch up with
yea's at the station later." Davis takes a step away
from the trailer, as Nelson and Barnes get back in
the suburban, start it up and pull away... trailer ramp
still down dragging the ground. Davis shouts,
"Hey!" The suburban stops and Barnes jumps out
of the passenger side and runs to the back of the
trailer, lifts and closes the ramp, then looks at Davis

and shrugs his shoulders as he returns to the vehicle.
Davis shakes his head as they pull away.

Returning to Debbie's office at the television
station, James eats a candy bar while looking
through Debbie's file drawers. The door opens and
James slams the drawer shut, and turns quickly to
see Debbie standing with a small box in her hands
staring at him curiously. She asks, "Find what you
were looking for?" James replies, "I just uh, dropped my
candy bar." James nods toward the file cabinet then
continues, "How did it go?" She sighs then shuts the door
and sets the box on her desk. James takes the box and
opens it, while finishing with his candy bar. "You got it."
He closes the box and takes it, then
stands in front of Debbie smiling.
"Don't get caught with it, Ok? I could lose my
job if you do," says Debbie. James replies,
"Don't you worry about a thing sweetness."
They lean in and kiss for a moment. "I'll be home
around eight, Ok ," says James.
"Ok," replies Debbie. They kiss briefly and
James exits the office quickly.

Outside in the station parking lot, James gets in
his van and starts it up. He adjusts his rear view
mirror, and notices the two men from earlier sitting
in a black SUV across the Street watching him. He
starts to whistle as he puts it in gear and pulls out of
the parking lot towards the two men. As James
passes right next to them, he smiles and waves.
"Hey! How's it hanging," he shouts, as they pull
out and follow him. James looks in the rear view
mirror and says, "So you boys wanna play huh?"

20

James turns on the radio full blast playing Heavy
Metal music, then floors it. The SUV floors it right
through a red light almost hitting two cars, honking
from all directions. James runs through another red
light, zig zagging through cross traffic. The SUV
approaches the intersection and partially locks up
the brakes, sliding sideways then regaining control
in pursuit of James...more horns honking.
James looks in his rear view and says,
"Not bad, lets see how you handle this?"
James whips into an alley. An old bum sits in the alley
wearing an old trench coat and a cap, drinking a bottle of
whiskey. James speeds by him and just misses him.
"Sorry!" Shouts James. The bum ignores him and puts the
bottle to his mouth, when suddenly the SUV whips into the
alley and also just misses the
bum, causing the bum to drop the bottle and break.
The bum looks in their direction and drunkenly
shouts, "Somoma bitches!" James passes a dumpster on
wheels and locks up the brakes to a screeching halt. He
jumps out of the van and runs up to the dumpster, then
pushes the dumpster into the middle of the alley. Finishing,
he runs back into the van and peels away. The SUV locks
up the brakes and stops just tapping the dumpster. The man
driving pounds the steering wheel and growls aloud,
"Arrrr!"
James still speeding away and jamming the radio,
looks once more in the rear view and says, "Mess
with the best...burn like the rest." He speeds away.
Meanwhile, the two men move the dumpster out of
the way and hear the sound of metal scraping the
ground. They look behind them and see the bum
dragging a trashcan, walking towards them. The
bum picks up the can over his head, and staggers

backwards falling to the ground, with the can knocking him out. After seeing the bum knock himself out, they look at each other blankly.

CHAPTER 3
ABDUCTION

At a local gas station, James pulls in and stops at the pumps. An elderly man, Max, Caucasian, 60's, wearing overalls and a baseball cap, wiping his hands with a rag approaches James.

"How much today Mr. Lowery?" James replies, "Filler up Max." James hands Max his credit card, and Max begins to fill up the tank. James opens the box Debbie gave him, and pulls out a digital police scanner. He turns it on and flips through the channels. After a moment, he finds a live channel and tunes it in. Nelson's voice, "We're almost back from the Taylor ranch now… over." Dixie's voice replies, "Affirmative." James turns off the scanner and stares forward for a moment. He then leans out the window towards Max. "Say Max?" Max Replies, "Yes Mr. Lowery?" "How would I get to the Taylor ranch from here?" Max finishes with the gas pump, and approaches James, handing him his credit card back.

"You talkin bout Jessie's Place?"

"Yeah, Jessie's place."

"Well, just take Main here due East as fur as you can go, then take a right. Yea can't miss it."

"Thanks Max." James smiles and starts up the van, then flips a quarter to Max. Max catches it as James pulls away.

"Thanks," shouts Max as he waves to James.

On the dirt road leading to the Taylor ranch, James speeds down the road jamming to the music with a long dust cloud behind him. Davis's car approaches from ahead of him. They finally pass each other, and Davis looks in his rear view mirror, "Lowery! Shit!"

Davis whips his car around, turns on the lights and
sirens, and pursues James. James still speeding
down the road and jamming to the radio doesn't
notice Davis pursuing him. Davis on the bull horn,
"Lowery! Pull over! Now!" James still doesn't notice or
hear Davis as he pulls into the Taylor's driveway and stops
just eight yards from the mobile home. He turns off the
radio then the van. The pre-ignition kicks in briefly, then
stops with a bang. Davis stops right behind him and shuts
off his car, then steps out and walks up towards James.
James exits the van with a camera around his neck, and a
pad and pencil in hand. "Lowery," Davis says aloud. James
turns to
Davis and says, "Oh hi Chief. What brings you out
this way?"
"That's funny Lowery. I was just about to ask
you the same thing."
"Well, you know…just doing my job as a public
servant."
"Is that so? Well let me be the first to inform you,
you're not going to find anything out here. In fact…
why don't you tell me what led you out here in the
first place?"
"Look Chief. I'm not looking for any trouble.
I'm just going on a hunch is all."
The sun begins to set, as the stars become more and
more visible. "Well your hunch was wrong Lowery. So
pack it up and move it on out." Davis looks towards the
horizon behind the ranch, and his eyes widen.
James turns and looks, and his eyes widen as well.
Both their jaws drop at the same time, as they just
stare in awe at a bright metallic UFO, hovering
slowly towards them measuring approximately
twenty-five yards across, twelve yards in height,

and fifty yards off the ground.

"Are you seeing what I'm seeing," asks Davis.

"Yeah, incredible isn't it?" James drops his pad and pencil, then begins taking pictures. Davis slowly puts his hands on James' shoulder and says, "Lowery? We've gotta get out of here, now."

"Are you kidding? This is my ticket to Stardom.
I wouldn't miss this for the World!" James continues snapping away, as the UFO gets closer. Davis tugs on James' arm. "Come on Lowery! Now!"
James doesn't budge as he continues snapping
pictures. Davis angrily shouts, "Damn you Lowery!" He runs away to his car, gets in it and tries to start it, but no power source what so ever. The gates of the entrance and both vehicles begin to shake and shutter. Davis tries his shoulder radio, "Nelson! Come in!" A brief moment and no reply. Heavy winds suddenly all around. Davis gets out of his car and shouts at James, "Lowery! Come on!" James quickly turns to run towards Davis, and in doing so drops his camera, as a blue beam of light suddenly shines down on him, freezing his movement. James just stares at Davis with widened eyes and slurs,

"Chief?" Davis pulls out his gun and begins shooting at the UFO and yelling, "Ahhhhh! Ahhhhh!" The UFO now completely over James, shoots a small blue laser beam at Davis's gun, shooting it clean out of his hand some fifty yards away. Davis stops yelling and stares for the moment, as James is lifted up into the UFO by the blue beam. With James clearly out of sight, the blue beam disappears and Davis turns and runs away as fast as he can. He suddenly trips on a rock in the
middle of the driveway, and falls to his stomach, then covers his face as the UFO dives downward towards

him. He lies still as if dead. Just ten feet off the ground, the UFO right over Davis, suddenly climbs upward at an incredible speed and out of sight. Davis stands up and looks around for a moment, and his car lights suddenly come on. He looks carefully at his car, then slowly gets in and tries the ignition. It starts.

"Yeah," he shouts as he puts it in gear and does a one eighty peeling away from the ranch.

Inside the police department, Nelson, Barnes, and the two men in shades are sitting down at the desk in the lobby. The entrance door opens and Davis walks in, face and clothes dirty. He stops and faces everyone. "Sir? These gentlemen are with the government, and they've been waiting to see you," says Nelson. Davis takes off his hat and addresses the two men. "What part of the government do you men represent?" The leader of the two speaks, "The one which is considered of the utmost priority."

"National Security. So… what are you men of utmost priority looking for?"

"We're interested in a certain individual by the name of James Lowery." Davis briefly laughs then replies, "You're not gonna find him. Least not anytime soon." The two men briefly look at each other, then the man asks, "And why is that Chief Davis?"

Davis takes a few steps to the water cooler and turns his back to fill a glass of water, and a long wide burn mark from his buttocks to the top of his head is present, along with a missing patch of his hair. Everyone stands to stare at Davis, and the two men take off their sunglasses to see Davis's backside more closely. Davis continues, " Because he's

gone…far gone. And where to, I wouldn't know where to begin." Davis turns around with the glass of water and sips, then stops to see everyone staring at him. "Chief?" Nelson slowly and briefly directs his finger at Davis's back.
"What?" Davis asks as silence fills the room. He briefly looks behind him and says aloud, "Well? What is it?" The two men look at each other, nod their heads, and then look at Davis again.

A strange humming noise fills the interior of the UFO, as James lays unconscious only wearing his boxers, on a table tucked away in one of the UFOs compartments. Both of his wrists and ankles bound by metal restraints. An alien, approximately five feet tall, bluish gray skin tone wearing a light gray body suit, a very slender build with a large pear shape head, large upward slanted eyes, a tiny slit for a mouth, and tiny holes for both nose and ears gracefully approaches James. The alien holding a small cylindrical chrome type of device gently places it on James' forehead. The device lights up brightly, but briefly. The alien removes it and James wakes up suddenly, startled with fear and gasping. He looks at the alien and starts to panic. "Who are you? What have you done to me? Where am I?" The alien replies in English, with a style and voice that sounds like a four-year-old on a sugar high, "Do not be frightened. We mean no harm to you." James refrains from his panic and stares at the alien. "If that were the case…why am I strapped to this table? Hey…you speak English." The alien smiles and says, "Yes. For many of your centuries we have adapted the use of your culture

28

with our own. Necessary for communicable relations."
James in awe just staring at the alien asks, "Who are you?"
The alien smiles again and addresses himself, "I am Deek."
Deek addresses James, "And you?"
"Scared shitless. That's what I am."
"Do not worry Mr. Shitless." James responds quickly, "No no no. Lowery. My name is James Lowery."
"A pleasure it is to have you with us Mr. Lowery. We have long searched for a subject of your nature to conduct non extinction process." James' eyes glare at Deek with total curiosity and worry. "What do you mean by subject, and extinction?" Deek replies, "Your genetic culture is of one among billions. Harness it we shall, to save life."
"What your saying, is I'm gonna be some sort of experiment, to save what life?"
"Your world Mr. Lowery."
James' eyes widen as he asks, "My world? What's wrong with my world…Earth?"
"The race known as the Tre'toan, a virus they have released. Soon spread it will, until your kind exist no more."
"Your serious, aren't you?" Deek simply gestures with a nod. "I've a lot of questions for you, Deek. But first, could you let me up off this damn table, and bring me my clothes?"
Deek smiles again and waves the little cylindrical device over the restraints, and they receded into the table. "Apologize we do Mr. Lowery."
James sits up and rubs his wrist, as another alien approaches with James' clothes.
James briefly bows to the alien, and the alien returns his gesture, then sets James' clothes on the table and walks away. James grabs his clothes and

begins dressing. "This is so unreal...any second now I'm gonna wake up." Suddenly the faint sound of a cow mooing. James briefly stops dressing and listens, then shakes his head and continues dressing.

CHAPTER 4
VIOLATION

Back at the police station, Davis now with a
change of clothes and cleaned up with a shaved
head, covered with a baseball cap, exits his office
and walks up to Nelson and Barnes playing cards
and drinking soda's. They look at Davis, and
Barnes comments, "Hey Chief... that cap looks
swell on ya." Nelson kicks Barnes in the leg and
Barnes looks at Nelson as Davis responds,
"As soon as you two are finished sitting around on
your butts, drinking soda's and making like the
streets are gonna patrol themselves?"
Nelson and Barnes both stand up quickly.
"Right away sir," says Nelson as he looks at
Barnes and they both walk away. Davis turns to
them. "Nelson?" Nelson and Barnes stop and turn
to him. "Yes Chief?" Replies Nelson. "Did you get a good
look at those men's identification?"
"Well... come to think of it sir...not really."
Davis moves his hands from his hips and crosses his
arms. "What do you mean not really Nelson?" Davis's tone
strengthens by the second. "Either you did...or you didn't."
Nelson removes his hat and replies,
"Well...no sir." Davis instantly showing the frustration of
Nelson and Barnes' incompetence, points his finger at both
of them. "You mean to tell me...that I just told
two men that no one knows who in the hell they
actually were...how to get to Lowery's house to do
who knows what to, to his wife possibly?"
Nelson and Barnes look at the floor with disgust, as
Davis continues, "And all because you two idiots
didn't check their Id's?" Davis quickly walks past them to
the entrance door, then turns to them and says aloud,
"Don't just stand their dipsticks!" Come on! "Davis opens
the door and exits, as Nelson and

Barnes follow. Davis's voice, "It's amazing you two even graduated kindergarten!"

A grandfather clock in James and Debbie's house presents the only sound heard with its hands reading eight fifty five. A sudden knocking on the door. Wearing jeans and a halter top, Debbie arrives in the foyer and immediately opens the door and says, "Where have," she stops and there stand the two yet unidentified men. "Mrs. Lowery I presume," asks the leader. "Yes. Who are you gentlemen? What do you want?"
"May we come in and talk with you Mrs. Lowery? It's a matter of national security." Debbie wears a look of curiosity as she asks, "First you tell me who you really are, and what this is about. Otherwise, I'm shutting the door." The men look at each other briefly, then the leader says, "I'm afraid I can't tell you just who we are, or discuss what needs to be discussed out here in the open of your dwelling." Debbie places her hand on the door and says, "Then I'm afraid I can't help you." She tries to close the door and the leader quickly stops her with his hand. "Hey! Who do you think you are?" Debbie tries one more time to close the door, buy can't. "Help! Help! Somebody help me," she shouts aloud with fright as the men force the door open, covering Debbie's mouth and nose with a cloth, and Debbie passes out as they quickly shut the door.
Aboard Alien Deek's ship, James fully dressed walks alongside Deek towards what appears to be the control bridge, filled with triangular shaped holographic monitors, displaying star systems, planets, and strange alien charts with shapes and

33

number sequences. James in total awe as he looks all around. "My God...unbelievable," says James as he continues his exploration of the incredibly advanced technology. Four more aliens present working touch activated control panels. There are also several luxurious chairs located around the center of the bridge. James stops walking and rests his hands on the backrest of one.

"So this is how they work. For that matter... evade all proof of existence man has ever so tried to reveal." Deek has a seat next to James still standing. Deek then nods to his alien companions, and they touch a panel, then small portions of the bridge wall approximately six feet wide by three feet tall, begin to slide side to side slowly revealing outer space, and stars streaking by traveling forward. James' eyes widen as he slowly walks towards the window. "No. It can't be." James arrives at their edge and just stares in disbelief. "Deek, just how far, and fast are we going?" Deek replies, "What is known to your people as light speed. Ten light years of travel we shall." Suddenly a man's voice with an English accent behind James, "So, what do you think?" James quickly turns to face a man about sixty years of age, clean cut gray hair, neatly trimmed beard, and wearing a white jumpsuit with his hands rested behind his back.

"Who in the hell are you? You look a little familiar." James tries to make him out. The man replies, "Landin Burke. It's a pleasure to meet you James." They briefly shake hands.

"Now I remember. Professor Landin Burke of the European Study for Aviation and Exploration. But...you suddenly turned up missing for no apparent reason some twenty years ago. Wow, it's a small Universe after all."

"I'd have to disagree with you on that comment." James briefly waves his hand and says, "Well yeah. So tell me professor… how did you come about… all of this?"

"It's quite a long story, one that I don't care to discuss. But I can tell you…that mine, and Deek's people's intentions are truly sincere…and if all goes well, we'll be able to put a stop to the Tre'toans dark plan to wipe out all mankind on Earth." James crosses his arms and says, "You know…you could've made my arrival here a little less, we'll, terrifying."

"What…and deny you the right of the total alien abduction experience? You should thank me." Burke looks at Deek and winks. Deek smiles. "Crap," says James. "What," asks Burke.

"I didn't get a chance to tell my wife I loved her."

"Don't worry James. I assure you, you'll be seeing her again soon. Why…she's probably cooking your dinner as we speak."

In front of James and Debbie's house in the darkness, Davis pulls up with his lights off and parks. Nelson and Barnes pull up in the Suburban and park with their headlights still on. Davis on his shoulder radio whispers coarsely, "Turn off your damn lights, now." Nelson's lights go off. Davis slowly gets out of his car and draws his gun, then jesters for Nelson and Barnes to come over to him. They exit the suburban and jog over to Davis. Davis whispers, "Listen close, and listen real good. I'm going to the front door, and then make my way in as quickly as possible. You two clowns are

gonna come in from the back on my signal. Got it?"
They nod and Davis goes towards the front door,
Nelson and Barnes to the back. At the front door,
Davis whispers into his shoulder radio, "I'm going in now."
Davis kicks the door open busting the door jam, and
running into the house with his gun pointed. In the back of
the house, Nelson and Barnes standing by the French doors
both counting, "One, two, three!" They both run and jump
into the French doors, knocking the doors down then
landing on top of them. Davis walks up to them and
holsters his gun. Nelson and Barnes stand up in pain,
rubbing their arms and heads. "At least you two can do one
thing right. Mrs.
Lowery's not here. No sign of struggle or
anything."
"Where do you suppose she is Chief," asks
Nelson. "We need to make some phone calls. I'll start
with the news station, while you two clean up this
damn mess."

   In the back seat of the two men's SUV, Debbie
lays bound in ropes and unconscious…the leader in
the passenger side, and the other driving on a
deserted highway. "She will prove vital to the
cause," say's the leader.
"Yes…she shall." The SUV speeds off into the
distance.

   Back aboard Deek's ship, James and Burke are
sitting down in the luxurious bridge chairs.
"So how did you know where to find me…out of
a billion people for that matter," asks James.
Burke smiles and replies, "You could say that
ninety nine percent of it was pure good old fashion

luck." Deek walks up to them and takes a seat, as
another alien enters and stops in front of them, with
a tray of what looks like a white glowing substance
in clear glasses. The alien serves them.

"What is this Professor," asks James as he slowly takes one
and carefully smells it. Burke and Deek drinking, Burke
replies, "Just a little concoction I developed, to strengthen
ones senses of inner well being." James sips it a little, then
tastes. "Tastes like…a White Russian?"

Burke smiles and says, "Yes…good isn't it?"

"First alien abduction…then I find out about
man's possible extinction, and me being a lab rat.
And now, I'm drinking White Russians traveling at
light speed to god knows where with a mad
Scientist, no offense…and you want my opinion
about a drink?"

"Think of this as a vacation…with a twist of
mystery and adventure."

"I get enough of that back home, thank you."

Burke sets his drink into a holder on a table between
them, then stands facing James. "Come…I'd like to
show you something?"

"Great. More surprises."

James sets down his drink and stands up to follow
Burke. They walk down a ramp into the lower half
of the ship. Once there, James looks at the Taylor's
laying down unconscious, fully clothed and
restrained. Overhead lights dimly light the room,
and alien medical equipment hangs from the ceiling
and walls. James walks up to the Taylor's.

"Who are these folks Professor?"

"As of right now, their contained evidence. I was
only borrowing," Suddenly a clear sound of a cow

mooing. James turns and takes a few steps and sees
a cow behind a set of bars, with suction cups
attached to its utters and eating hay. Burke finishes, "Their
cow."
"Now that's," James points at the cow, "Gotta
be a first!"
"Actually…it's not."
James turns to Burke and asks, "Tell me Professor… just
what sort of technique, was used on me…to find out about
my genetic cell structure,
as you would refer to?"
Burke briefly looks at the floor, then James, then
upwards at a series of long needles, long curved
shaft probes, and binding equipment, then back at
James. James looks upwards at the equipment and
passes out. "Now that's, a first, and the conclusion
of our tour."

   Davis driving his car in town pulls up to a stop
sign and puts his car in park, then stares forward for
a brief moment. He then uses his shoulder radio,
"Nelson? Come in Nelson." Nelson's voice,
"Yes Chief?"
"I've scoured every inch of this side of Town.
You boys find anything yet?"
"No Sir."
"All right. Keep looking. I'm gonna try out by
the dumps." Davis puts his car in gear and pulls away.

   With the time now being midnight, the black
SUV is parked at the City dump in front of a
portable trailer. Only one light on in the trailer,
visible all around the entire area as well. Inside the
dimly lit trailer, in an office with a bookshelf, three

chairs and a table, Debbie sits in one of the chairs across from the two men. Her arms crossed, and eyes squinting at them with a piercing stare. "Do you realize who I am…and the shit that's gonna hit the fan when I turn up missing," says Debbie with an authoritative tone. The leader takes off his glasses and leans forward in her face. "You should realize, that your petty words are a waste of your final breaths. Soon you will bare witness to the birth of a more deserving race than of your own…as we Tre'toans anticipate the annihilation of you discussing, and foul excuse of beings unworthy of inheriting this world." Debbie's eyes widen as the Tre'toan's eyes begin to glow red.

On the bridge of Deek's ship, Deek and his companions at the controls, as Burke stands over James who is sitting down unconscious. Burke lightly slapping James' face. "James…come on son. Snap out of it." James starts to come to, slowly opening his eyes. "What…what happened," says James with a groggy voice. Burke hands him a glass of water and a couple of pills. "Here you go. This will help you." James takes the water and the pills then asks, "What are these?"
"Simple ordinary aspirin. Don't you trust me?"
"Have I got a choice?"
James pops the aspirins in his mouth and gulps down the whole glass of water. He sets down the glass and sits up straight as Burke takes a seat next to him and says, "I had no idea a Supreme specimen of our race would be…how shall I put it…squeamish?"

"For your information Professor…it just so happens…that I earned every metal possible…in my Boy Scout Troop. It's just a little phobia I have about needles…and such."

"When and if we return safely to Silus, I'll be sure to administer a non…appalling approach upon the extraction process." James quickly looks at Burke with suspicion. "Wo wo wo! Lets back up to the part where you said…if we return. Just what are you, not telling me Professor?"

Burke sighs and replies, "Well…not to intentionally frighten you James, but judging by our previous location, I'd say we were smack dab in the middle of Tre'toan Space."

"Why in the hell of all places are we here?" James awaits an immediate response. "Relax James, we travel this route quite often. It's the quickest and safest route for that matter. And besides…the Tre'toans never pose as a threat at the speed we're traveling now."

Suddenly an eerie deep pulsating alarm sounds all over the ship. James' eyes widen, as Burke stands and looks at Deek. Deek says aloud to Burke, "Three vessels of Tre'toan origin approach in quadrant Alta!" James stands up and says aloud to Burke over the repetitive alarm, "I guess you could say you stand corrected!" Burke looks at James with haste as the ship suddenly shakes from a laser blast from the Tre'toan vessels. Burke and James both fall to the ground, James on his back, and Burke lying directly on top of James. James says while barely breathing, "Not my idea…of a good time."

"Don't worry…you're not my type."

Burke rolls off of James and stands up, then jogs over to Deek's side, as James sits up and re-gains his breath. "Strap yourself in James! We're about to engage in an intergalactic game of chess," shouts Burke. James quickly gets up and sits down strapping him-self in while saying, "Maybe they'd settle their differences over a White Russian!" Burke making trajectory adjustments with Deek replies, "Actually, their drink of choice, is blood!" James' eyes widen and brow's lift, as suddenly a small portion of the ceiling descends downward, revealing a gunnery station . The alarms finally stop sounding, as Burke runs towards the gunnery, when suddenly another hit from the Tre'toan's rocks the ship. Maintaining his balance, Burke gets into the seat of the gunnery station and straps himself in. Suddenly small blue beams from the ceiling shine down on Deek and his fellow Silustrians...a source of stationary support. Burke touches some shapes on the instrument panel, which light up upon doing so, and a hologram of the Tre'toan vessels appears...triangular in shape, slender in height, and deep black in color.

CHAPTER 5
INTRUSION

In space, Burke's and the Tre'toan's vessels still traveling at light speed, shifting in patterns side to side, and top to bottom in a cat and mouse chase, as laser fire exchange runs continuously. On the bridge of Burke's ship, Burke intently aiming and firing with the whole gunnery station pivoting back and fourth. "Hang tight James! I'm getting warmed up!" "We're gonna die," says James while leaning over covering his eyes. "Faith James! Have a little faith!"

On board one of the Tre'toan vessels, several Tre'toans dressed in black, sit at odd digital control panels, and one sits in a chair high above the rest. The interior resembles that of octagon shaped panels with lighted symbols flashing randomly. The Tre'toan Captain points forward. "Closer! We must destroy them before we enter Silustrian Space!"

Back on the bridge of Burke's ship, Burke still using the gunnery station, and James now with his fingers in his ears rocking back and forth repeating, "La la la la la." Burke carefully aiming on one of the Tre'toan vessels, "Come on...just a little bit more. Gotcha!" Burke fires and hits the center of the Tre'toan vessel's hull, blowing it to pieces. "Yes," shouts Burke.

Back at the dumps, Davis pulls up slowly and turns off his headlights, while stopping his car approximately fifty yards away from the SUV parked at the trailer. Noticing the SUV, Davis uses

his shoulder radio, "Nelson? Come in Nelson."
Nelson's voice, "Yes Chief?"
"I'm down at the dumps, and I found the SUV we've been looking for."
"We're on our way Chief."
"Good. Just keep your damn lights off when you get here."
"Yes Sir. Be there in about ten."
"Make it five Nelson."
"We'll try. Over and out."
Davis opens his glove compartment and pulls out a box of shotgun shells, then grabs a shotgun off his seat and begins loading the magazine chamber.

   Inside the trailer, Debbie still forced to sit in the chair, watching the Tre'toans holding an octagon shaped tray, with refractions of alien letters rising upward and vaporizing at their eye level. She leans forward. "How do I fit in to your evil scheme?" A moment, and no reply. She continues, "Hey…I'm talking to you bozo!" The leader looks at Debbie with his eyes glowing again and with a deep scratchy tone says, "Silence!" His eye's glow even brighter as Debbie begins to feel dizzy then suddenly passes out on to the table. He looks at his companion and his companion says,
"The element exists within her womb."
"Send the coordinates for our departure. Soon… we shall finally be rid of these humans, and ruling this new world along-side the Lord Zemious himself." He smiles.

   Davis sitting in his car tapping his fingers on the barrel of the shotgun impatiently. He looks at his watch and sighs, then says, "Screw it." He opens his door and exits quietly, then cautiously walks toward the trailer with his shotgun aimed. He reaches the trailer and looks in the windows, and sees movement…the Tre'toan's shadows. He then quietly walks up the steps and suddenly one of the steps creak. Davis freezes. Inside the trailer, the Tre'toans both turn their heads toward the door.

Outside the door, Davis tries the handle and it's unlocked. He slowly opens the door with a bit of door hinge creaking. The door fully open, Davis quickly jumps into the trailer with his shotgun drawn. He sees no one or thing yet, so he walks towards the back room, where the light escapes from under the door. He stops at the door when suddenly he is hit on the head from behind, his shotgun going off and falling to the ground, but not unconscious. He quickly turns towards the two Tre'toans and shouts, "Hey you son of bitches! Who do you think you are?"

The leader speaks, "We are the beginning, of your glorious ending…and you Chief Davis will further bare witness as well." Both their eyes begin to glow brightly as Davis briefly displays a frightful facial expression, then passes out.

Returning to our friends battling it out with the Tre'toans somewhere light years away from Earth, the cat and mouse chase continues with the two Tre'toan vessels pursuing. On the bridge of Deek's ship, James is slumped in his chair, eyes closed, squinting, and hands over his ears. Burke still firing at the Tre'toans, while Deek and companions control the ship. Suddenly another hit rocks the

ship, and Deek says aloud to Burke, "A fifty percent
loss of shielding, suffered we have."
"We should be close enough to alarm the guardian
fleet of our situation!" Deek nods and touches alien
letters to alert their guardian fleet for help. James
opens his eyes and removes his hands from his ears,
then looks at Burke, "Did you say fleet?" Burke still hard at
it with the shooting replies, "That you did!"
"Well in that case…is there anything I can do to
help?"
"Yes…you can stay put, and stay alive! If your
Dead, this entire venture would be for nothing!"
"Sounds good to me! You're doing just fine!"
Burke briefly looks at James with a sigh, and
continues his fighting. "Deek? When I say…go up
left down!"
Deek nods as Burke focuses. "Now!"
Viewing the battle in space, Deek maneuvers the
ship quickly to Burke's request and Burke fires
rapidly at one of the Tre'toan vessels, directly
hitting their bridge.

   On the bridge of the Tre'toan
vessel, the crew screams as a tremendous explosion
destroys the entire ship, and flaming debris flies
away revealing Burke's ship.

   Back aboard Burkes ship, Burke shouts, "Yes!
One more to go!"
"Yeah! Kicking some alien, I mean Tre'toan butt,"
shouts James as the Silustrian crew members look
at James, and he smiles widely then waves to them.

   It's nearly one am now at the trailer location, as

Nelson and Burke finally arrive with their lights off. They stop behind Davis's car and shut off the engine. Nelson uses his shoulder radio, "Chief?" A moment and no reply. Nelson tries again, "Chief …Come in Chief." Still no reply. "I don't see him in his car, and he's not answering," says Nelson.

"Where do you suppose he is," asks Barnes.

"He must be in there." Nelson and Barnes both looking at the trailer.

Inside the trailer, Davis still lays on the floor unconscious. The Tre'toans finish with the strange octagon tray device, and the leader folds it up and inserts it down the front of his pants. The grunt Tre'toan then lifts up Debbie, who still lays unconscious slumped over the table, onto his shoulder. The leader turns then walks out of the office, and the grunt carrying Debbie follows. Just outside the door of the trailer, Nelson and Barnes standing near the foot of the steps hear the Tre'toans walking towards the door. "There's two people," says Nelson.

"What if it's the Chief and Mrs. Lowery?"

"What if it's not?"

"What if it is?"

"But what if it isn't?"

"Is."

"Isn't."

"Is."

"Isn't"

Suddenly they see the doorknob begin to turn. Nelson and Barnes run away to the corner of the trailer and peek around the corner. The Tre'toans step out of the door with Debbie still on the grunt's

shoulder. They stop and turn facing Nelson and
Barnes. Nelson and Barnes keep tucked behind the
corner and look at each other while drawing their
guns and counting to three. On three they jump out
with their guns drawn, and the doors on the SUV
shut as it starts up and peels away. "Shoot!
They're getting away," says Barnes as they holster
their guns. "The Chief," says Nelson as they run up the
steps and quickly push the door open. A thud noise and
Davis's voice, "Damn it!"
In the trailer on the floor, Davis sits up holding his
nose and looks at Nelson and Barnes.
"Before this is over, remind me to pull my boots
out of your asses!" Nelson and Barnes rush to his aid, but
Davis holds up his hand to stop them.
"Stop! Nelson, give me your gun?"
Nelson briefly looks at Barnes and back to Davis.
"Why do you need my gun Sir?" Davis stands
up. "So I can shoot your dumb asses!"

  Returning to the galactic chess game, the zig
zagging and laser fire continues. On Burke's bridge,
Deek and crew remain at their posts, as Burke
remains in the gunnery firing, and James seated
watching the hologram, as the Tre'toan vessel fires
directly towards the bridge. Laser fire hit's them,
breaking through the shields and damaging the
gunnery station as sparks and smoke emit all around
Burke. Electricity out of the console suddenly
shocks Burke, and knocks him out. James looks at
Deek and Deek says, "Worry not Mr. Lowery…
fleet arrived it has!" James turns and looks toward
the windows to see dozens of UFOs approaching
from all directions.

48

In space, the Tre'toan vessel alters its course quickly, but is destroyed by several of the Silustrian ships laser fire. The Silustrian ships then assume an escort position around Burke's ship, as they slow to mach speed. On Deek's bridge, the blue overhead containment beams disappear, and one of the crew walks over to Deek and takes over the controls. Deek quickly walks over to Burke who is still knocked out. James struggles briefly with his seat belt, freeing himself and running over to Burke. James unbuckles Burke, and Deek helps James lift him out of the gunnery and lay him down on the floor of the ship. Another Silustrian crew member walks up with a small round shiny disk, and slowly waves it over Burke's head. Everyone kneeling beside Burke, as his eyes suddenly open.

"That was a close one," says Burke as he slowly rises while rubbing the back of his neck.

"We're safe now Professor. Their fleet's here," says James with a look of relief. "I see what you mean now…by enough of this entertainment back home," says Burke with a grin. James lends Burke his hand and helps him to his feet while saying, "But this, is way off the charts!"

CHAPTER 6
TRANSITION

Speeding down the dark desert highway, are Nelson and Barnes' Suburban. Nelson driving, Davis riding shotgun with a shotgun, and Barnes in the back seat leaning forward between them. "How do ya know they didn't double back to Town Chief," Nelson asks.
"Ok Nelson...here's an IQ test for ya. If you kidnapped a woman, and zapped a police officer with your eyes, where would you most preferably high tale it to?" Nelson thinking as Barnes says, "I know the," Davis interrupts, "Shut up Barnes!" Barnes' eyes widen as he slowly leans back in his seat. Davis continues with Nelson, "Well...come on Sherlock! You don't know do ya?" After a moment of Nelson trying his hardest to answer Davis, Davis adds,
"That's why I'm a Chief...and both of you two clowns, are clowns!"

Also on the dark desert road miles ahead of Davis's posse, the black SUV driven by the Tre'toans also speeds down the road. The grunt at the wheel, the leader riding shotgun, and Debbie in the backseat laying down unconscious. She begins to wake up, slowly opening her eyes, and careful not to make any sudden movements. She slowly slides her legs off the seat and onto the floorboard. The leader briefly looks back at Debbie, and she closes her eyes remaining still. After a moment, she opens her eyes again, and slowly rises up behind the driver seat. She suddenly starts choking the grunt and the SUV weaves all over the road as him and the leader struggle with Debbie.
"Stop the vehicle!" Shouts the leader, and the

grunt slams on the brakes, sliding all over the road for a moment, then finally coming to a stop sideways. Debbie quickly releases the grunt, opens the door, then jumps out and runs into the desert hills. Both the Tre'toans exit the SUV, then walk toward Debbie's direction. Their eye's light up red like flashlights, scanning the hillside as they walk.

   Returning to deep space ten light years away, Deek and the rest of his fellow Silustrian's UFOs approach a planet that looks similar to Earth, but three moons of different proportion and color exist among the planet's outer origin. An orange sun burns brightly in the distance.
Aboard Burke's ship on the bridge, James and Burke stand by the bridge window viewing the totally new and fascinating world in James' eyes for the first time. James in complete and total disbelief, leans against the windowsill and says, "Wow...I never knew such another world like this could exist."
"Besides having three moons instead of just one... Silus is also four times the mass that of Earth."
James turns with excitement to Burke,
"Plenty of elbow room...hey Professor?"
James performs a little elbow routine, then returns to the view of Silus as they draw closer to the illustrious beautiful New World.
Just a quarter of a mile high above a city on Silus looking down, dozens of beautifully crafted architectural buildings and sculptures similar to Earth's ancient architecture, fill seventy percent of the landscape. The rest of the surroundings compiled with lush green trees, water fountains,

hillsides as far as the eyes can see, and dozens of
UFOs of all different shapes and sizes flying
around. Burke's ship and the fleet fly downward towards an
enormous round landing platform, located in the center of
the city atop a round spiral building.
Landing indicator lights that flash into lighted rings
appear all over the landing port. Still looking out the
window of Burke's ship, James and Burke remain leaning
on the sill next to one another. James looks all around in
amazement and says, "It's the most beautiful thing I've
ever seen." James looks at Burke to add, "Besides my wife
that is." James turns back to the window as the ship stops
and begins to land.
"Silus has many things more beneficial than
Earth. One of them, being its pollution free air.
Wait till you get a breath of that in your carbonated
lungs."
"What a story this could be," James whispers as Burke
looks at him. "Did you say story," Burke asks with
curiosity. "Just talking to myself is all," James replies as
Burke nods and pats James on the shoulder. "Come on lad.
We've got fish to fry."
Burke and James walk away.

  Back on the desert road, Davis and posse pull up
to the stranded SUV parked in the middle of the
road. Everyone exits quickly to positions behind
their doors, guns drawn.
"Go ahead Nelson, say I told ya so." Says Davis
sarcastically.
"Barnes, you watch our six while we move in.
And remember one thing, no matter what...do not
look into their eyes. Understand?" They answer,
"Understand."

"Good, lets do this."
Davis looks at Nelson, Nelson appearing nervous as
all hell, and gestures to move in. They both ease
out from behind the doors, guns aimed at the SUV,
and slowly approach it. Making it all the way up to
the SUV safe so far, Davis whips the barrel of his
shotgun into the driver side only to see it empty. He
lowers his shotgun and turns around to see Nelson
shaking so much, his gun could drop at any second.
"Boy…you look like a wet dog on a cold winters
night." Davis begins to laugh, and then Barnes laughs for a
moment. They finish laughing as Nelson
lowers his gun and calms down.
"All right you two, time to get down to business.
I'm gonna head up over that way,"
Davis points in Debbie's last known direction,
"And you two head over that way. If you spot our
Suspects, or Mrs. Lowery, stay put and radio
Me, quietly. Can you handle that?"
They both nod. "If you screw this up, you boys
are gonna either get yourselves killed, or end up
flippin burgers down at the burger ranch." Davis
slings his shotgun over his shoulder and walks
away. Nelson and Barnes shut the doors to the
Suburban and walk away.

   Deep in the desert hills of the pitch black night,
Debbie about out of breath and struggling to keep a
steady pace through the rugged terrain, stops to look
behind her gasping with a look of fear, and sees the
red beams of light from the Tre'toan's eyes getting
closer. She turns and continues her quest to safety.
The Tre'toans keep tracking her steadily.

Back on Silus in the lower deck of Burke's ship, James looks at the floor in fear of looking up and seeing the needles and probes again. Burke is packing a satchel with medical and chemical items. James glances over at the Taylors and says, "What's gonna happen to those old folks Professor?"

"They'll be just fine. They're in a bit of a hibernation sleep for the moment. They'll be returning to Earth as well." The cow moos.

"What about our furry companion?"

The cow chomping on hay.

"I suppose, that it would be of her own decision." James briefly wears a curious look, as Burke finishes with packing his satchel and turns to James. "Are you ready to take that big step for Mankind," says Burke as he gestures with his Hand, and a large portion of the floor begins to descend, forming an entrance ramp.

"After you, I insist," Replies James with a brief hand gesture of his own. "All right …as you wish." Burke begins to walk down the ramp, and James follows. Just outside the ship, the fleet ships docked, entrance ramps down and all aliens exiting the ships as Burke and James exit and stop at the foot of the ramp. James looking around taking a deep breath through his nose then exhales slowly, "Ahhhhh." Burke looks at James with a smile, "Well?" James takes another deep breath and exhales then looks at Burke, "Yeah!"

"Exactly my thoughts as well, upon my first arriving."

"It's so…pure. You could market it!"

"The only problem with that idea, is your ten light years away."

"That would be a bit of a problem."
Deek casually walks down the ramp, as the dozens
of other UFO crewman walk by James and Burke,
smiling and briefly waving to them. James notices
in the distance, women Silustrians approaching
while smiling, but are dressed in different color skin
tight suits...and to his surprise, he can't help but
notice a distinct difference in the proportion of their
groins. James looks curiously at Deek, then Burke.
"Professor...is Deek...well...you know,"
he asks in a low tone. Burke looks at James
with a grin, "A bit obvious, isn't it?"
Burke chuckles briefly and adds with a low tone,
"Believe it or not, of the male gender he is...just the
opposite biologically." James' eyes briefly widen.
"Wow, bizarre. But hey, each to his...or her
own." Burke takes a step and turns to James.
"Come, I'll introduce you to the Queen."
James' eyes widen again briefly as he answers,
"Queen? All right." James, Burke and Deek begin walking
away and Burke places his hand on James' shoulder and
says, "The Queen is going to enjoy making your
acquaintance." James looks at Burke inquisitively.

  Back in the dark hills of the Arizona desert, Davis
now deep in the hills, uses his shoulder radio,
whispering, "Nelson?"
"Yes Sir," Nelson speaks aloud.
"Damn it Nelson... keep it down," Davis whispers
coarsely. Nelson responds, "Yes Sir. Sorry Sir," Nelson
whispers.
"You two find anything yet?"
"No Sir."

"Well, keep at it...over and out." Davis
continues his search, pressing forward to save
Debbie.

  Debbie strung out and about to collapse suddenly
slips and falls down a slope of small rocks, sliding
and screaming as she goes. She finally stops
sliding and screaming, only to come face to face
with a black scorpion. She freezes still and just
stares with a look of fright, then ever so slowly
begins to back away from it. The red lights of the
persistent Tre'toans eyes, are again visible to
Debbie from above her location. She quickly rises
to her feet and continues to trek her way to safety.
The Tre'toans Stop and turn off their glowing red
eyes, then the leader takes out the octagon tray. He
holds it level in the center of his hands, and it folds
itself out to full size. It suddenly lights up brightly,
and the strange refractive letters and shapes begin to
rise from it. Davis only about a hundred yards
away, notices the light beam produced by the
Tre'toan device. He stops in his tracks and uses his
shoulder radio.
"Nelson? Come in!"
"Yes Chief," Nelson whispers.
"Work your way back over towards me. And
hurry! I think I found our suspects."
"We're on our way Chief."
Davis aims his shotgun and walks toward the beam
of light.

  Back on Silus in a long and narrow glass tunnel,
James, Burke and Deek stand in place as they are
escalated to their first destination, the Queen's

Temple. Across from them, James can't help but
notice a human couple. While staring at them
James asks, "Are they from, Earth?"
"If I said no...I'd be lying."
"How many more of us are here Professor?"
"Oh...about a million...give or take a few."
James looks at Burke, "How is that possible?"
"Simple...we humans have been coming to Silus
for centuries. So if you did your homework
correctly...you would assume the same equation."
"You're the scientist."
"Yes...so nice of you to remind me."
They finally arrive at the opening of an ovular
shaped hall. They all walk into the hall, a beautiful
tall structure, with pillars about its walls. Dozens of
Silustrians standing, turn and face James, Burke and
Deek. They all bow briefly, as James, Burke and
Deek stop and bow in return. They continue walking
forward, and just ahead of them, the Queen,
Mirla...appearing to look half Silustrian and half human
with beautiful big blue eyes, proportioned like a model,
wearing a silver tiara, and dressed in a purple gown. She
sits on a luxurious throne comprised of a velvet type of
material. Two Silustrian woman also in dresses stand on
each side of her. James, Burke and Deek stop before her
and bow briefly. Mirla displays an instant interests for
James upon seeing him. Burke begins the introductions,
"Your Highness...always a pleasure to be in your
presence." Burke takes her hand and briefly kisses
it. James just standing still holding his hands, and
noticing the way Mirla stares at him with a smile.
He tries to avoid her stare without being rude at the
same time. Mirla stands while smiling at James,

58

and her height is five foot eight. She approaches
James with her hand out. "Your Highness, I present to
you…James Lowery." Burke finishes with the introduction.
James looks at Burke, and Burke signals James to take her
hand and kiss it. James briefly tightens his lips, then looks
at Mirla still smiling, and takes her hand and quickly
kissing, then releasing it.
"I am Mirla, and you must be the supreme human
the professor has long been searching for. It's quite
an honor to meet you James." Mirla's voice as of a
humans, and very soft. James responds, "My pleasure as
well your Highness. You'll have
to pardon any rudeness I may present…this is all so
new to me." Mirla looks at James with a seductive
smile, as she ever so slowly walks around James,
observing him, and lightly caressing his shoulders
and back. James looks at Burke with the widest
eyes ever, as a plea for help. Burke tries his hardest
to contain a smile and refrain from laughing. Mirla
finishes her observation of James, standing in front
of him. "Yes…indeed you are a supreme
specimen."
"Me? Na," says James while shaking his head.
"Tell me James…have you a companion back
Home," she asks with a sexy wink. James instantly
holds his hand up to show his wedding ring.
Pointing at it with a smile he replies, "Happily married,
see?" Mirla smiles and says, "She's quite a fortunate
woman." Mirla sits back down and adds,
"I would be as well. I look forward to having
you…for dinner this evening." James' eyes widen again, as
he swallows hard and says, "For dinner…swell."
Burke takes a step forward, " If you'll excuse us

59

now your Highness…we've a lot of work to get started on." Burke briefly bows, then James and Deek as well. They turn and walk away.

James addresses Burke quietly, "Why didn't you warn me?"

"I thought you handled the situation rather well… don't you?"

"No thanks to your silence."

They continue walking away.

CHAPTER 7
EXTRACTION

Still in the dark desert ravine, Debbie now strung out and dehydrated, struggles on her feet to evade the Tre'toans. She suddenly drops to her knees from exhaustion, and looks behind her. She sees nothing but the dark ravine, and its illuminated shadows cast from the setting moon. She then decides to sit down and rest for a while.

Davis crouched down and walking slowly with his shotgun aimed, approaches the Tre'toans from approximately forty feet away. He stops and takes cover behind a boulder, watching the Tre'toans holding the strange device. He looks carefully all around them, but doesn't notice Debbie anywhere. The Tre'toans suddenly stop with the device and the leader puts it away again down his pants.

Davis uses his shoulder radio, "Nelson, come in," he whispers.

"Yes Chief," Nelson whispers.

"I found them…but Mrs. Lowery's not with them. What's your location?"

"We're approaching the vehicles just now."

"Oh hell, I need you two to put it in gear and get your asses up here ASAP."

"You mean as soon as possible Chief?"

"Yes Nelson!"

Davis realizing he may have been heard, looks around the edge of the rock and notices the Tre'toans walking his way. Davis quickly leans his back against the rock, and exhales long while hugging his shotgun, then looks up to the sky. "Don't fail me now Lord…please don't fail me now." Davis takes several deep breaths quickly, psyching himself up to confront them, then with lightening speed whips out from behind the rock,

positioning the shotgun dead aimed at the two.
"Freeze you son of a bitches!" They freeze.
"And don't you think about pulling any of that red
eye shit with me either…or the Coyotes'll be lickin
your brains up off the ground. Ya dig?"
The leader smiles and replies, "The simple truth being
somewhat of a disappointment for you to digest Chief
Davis…is even if you were to end our lives…nothing can
save yours, or any of your people from the
inevitable deaths you so truly deserve."
Davis switching aim from head to head, "I'll be the judge
of that! Now tell me where Mrs. Lowery is! You've got
five seconds!" A brief moment goes by as the Tre'toans
just smile. "This is your last warning! Where is she?"
Suddenly a large rock hits the grunt Tre'toan in the back of
the head, and he goes down to the ground unconscious. The
leader jerks his head to look behind him, and sees Debbie
holding another one. Debbie stands still with an angry
stare, as the
leader grits his teeth with anger. Davis still aiming
his shotgun and Debbie says, "I've had about all I'm gonna
take from you assholes anymore." Davis shouts to Debbie,
"Mrs. Lowery, it's Ok now! Come on over to me! He so
even twitches, he's road kill!"
Debbie runs over to Davis and stands behind him.
The leader staring at them with intense anger.
Says, "You're making the last mistake you ever
will." While no one pays attention to the grunt on
the ground, he opens his eyes and looks at Davis
and Debbie as his eyes begin to glow red. Davis
catches it in time and takes aim at him, then pulls
the trigger, blowing off the top of his head. The
grunt squeals with a shrieking sound for one
moment then dies. "I warned em about that red shit,"

says Davis, still aimed at the leader.

"Now you've done it, says the leader, and suddenly seeing something the size of a fist, tries to force its way out of the rear end of the grunts pants. It punches and hisses at the same time. Davis and Debbie watching it and the leader is smiling again.

Debbie appearing frightened again as Davis asks the leader, "What is that!" The leader replies, "Why don't you ask it yourself, Chief Davis?" Suddenly the strange creature busts upward out of the grunt's rear end, resembling a long slimy slug, with legs like a centipede, horns like a beetle, teeth like a piranha, and glowing red. It flexes like a King Cobra and screeches. Debbie screams, as Davis keeps his aim on the leader. The creature then begins to move towards Davis and Debbie, and just before it comes within four yards of them, Davis shoots a round into it, blowing it in half, as it screeches briefly to its death. Davis quickly cocks the shotgun and aims it at the leader, as he tries to take a step forward with his teeth gritting stare again. "From what I've just seen…you must be from the planet hemorrhoid," says Davis to the leader. "You fail to amuse me with your lame and meaningless insinuations!"

"Your ass is fixin to be lame, just like your slimy friend, if you don't start talking and tell me where the hell your space ship took this ladies husband!" Debbie looks at Davis with question, "Space ship, James? What are you talking about Chief?"

Somewhere around the location of the scene, Nelson and Barnes are jogging, tired and gasping.

They stop and lean over to catch their breaths.
"I'm telling ya… it came from that direction,"
says Nelson as he briefly points.
"I sure hope your right. The Chief's going to have our
butt's…cookin burgers if you're wrong."

   Davis finishing his explanation to Debbie, while
still aimed at the leader.
"And that's the way it went down…didn't it
snake ass?"
"Enough of this," The leader says aloud as he
reaches into his pants.
"Stop, or I'll blow your damn head off,"
shouts Davis as the Leader's eyes light up red,
and he pulls out the device. Davis shoots and
blows a huge hole through his head. The leader
drops to the ground like a side of beef. Davis looks
at Debbie, "Run!"
"Why, you've got a gun." Suddenly another creature begins
to work its way out of the leader's rear end.
"I'm out of ammo," says Davis.
"That's a good reason."
They both run away as the creature exits the leader.

   Returning to Silus, James, Burke, and Deek walk
through the illustrious City streets filled with aliens
and humans, strolling along, working in shops,
shopping and etc.
"It looks like everyone's, one big happy family,"
says James while observing his entire
surroundings. "Yes, and you'll also notice, no policeman
patrolling the streets…no hustle and bustle of congested
traffic or crowd's of people. And most
importantly…no crime what so ever. Hard to

believe isn't it?"

"Not from what I've seen so far. In fact we could use a huge dose of this back home." Burke laughs briefly and says, "Yes...quite a difference it would make." Deek looks at James and says, "A sadness however, several Earthlings understand not the importance of peace, and tranquility." Burke responds, "In due time Deek...in due time." They come to a three story building round in structure, white in color, with domes extruding upwards from its roof. Burke steps up to a chrome doorway and stops, then turns facing James and Deek. The door opens upward and Burke gestures to James, "You first this time James...I insist." James checking the place out asks, "What is this place?"

"My home," replies Burke with a proud smile.

"Your home...looks more like an observatory."

"Well, to a degree...thus also being the truth. Shall we?" Burke gestures again, then James and Deek walk in with Burke following them.

Back home, Debbie and Davis run through the dark hills, as the Tre'toan creature still glowing with its illumines red color and hissing, snakes its way along the ground at a comparable speed to Debbie and Davis's. Davis right behind Debbie uses his shoulder radio, "Nelson, Barnes, we're being chased by...something...I can't explain! Are you their Nelson?" Nelson and Barnes standing on top of a ridge, listening to Davis panic for help. Nelson on his shoulder radio replies while looking at Barnes, "We hear you Chief! Where are you?"

"We're headed back to the road, hurry up,"
Davis's voice replies gasping for air.
"We can't screw this up Barnes. Let's go!"
They both take out their pistols and run towards the
road.

   While Debbie and Davis still run from the
Tre'toan creature, she stumbles and falls face first
to the ground. Davis quickly stops and kneels
down to help her back up, and suddenly a long and
eerie hiss is heard behind them. Debbie sits up as
Davis slowly turns his head and sees the creature
just seven feet behind them, coiled up like a
cobra ready to attack. Debbie and Davis remain
calm, as Davis slowly grabs his shotgun, then
suddenly slings it at the creature, hitting the
creature in the side of the head, but doing no
damage what so ever. The creature shrieks loudly
as Debbie picks up her rock again and secretly
gives it to Davis from behind him. He chucks it as
hard as he possibly can right at the creatures face,
and the creature opens its mouth wide and catches
it in its mouth. The rock begins to glow. The
creature then chomps down on the rock, and it
shatters into pieces. The creature then smiles.
"Oh shit," says Davis. They quickly get to their feet and
run like hell.

   Back on Silus In Burke's lavishly furnished home,
adorned with ancient art, tapestries, and photos of man's
historic discoveries in space, Burke stands behind a bar of
what appears to consist of black marble. He pours drinks,
as James looks at the photographs. Deek then walks up to
Burke and stops.

Burke looks at Deek and quietly says, "Prepare for the extraction. We'll be along shortly." Deek nods and walks behind the bar, where an exit ramp going downward awaits him. Deek enters the exit ramp, and the exit ramp closes into the floor. Burke walks over to James and holds out a drink to give him. "Drink?" James turns around and curiously takes the drink while replying, "Is this another one of your homemade concoctions?" James smells it briefly and Burke replies, "Actually it isn't, It's Silustrian Ale." James sips it and says, "Hmm. Not bad, not too bad at all. So Professor...I presume that since we're in no immediate danger, you'll tell me about this virus, that's threatening Earth as we speak?"

"Let's have a seat, shall we?" Burke gestures James to sit on a round luxurious black leather couch. They both sit down and Burke opens the conversation, "It started some thousand years ago...War between Silus and Tre'toa. Strangely, the Tre'toans idea of peace and harmony, was to have complete control of Silus' activity's with other worlds." Burke takes a drink and continues, "But of course, Silus wouldn't comply to such an outrageous, and mad request. So...the war began, and now...Earth is the Tre'toan's prime source of showing Silus its devilish capabilities. Ending all human life on Earth, and posing more of a threat by inhabiting it...for further empowering forces of evil." James just staring blankly at Burke, takes a big gulp of his drink then asks, "Where on Earth... the location, did they release the virus Professor? And how are we gonna stop it in time?"

"Sadly, we don't know the exact location of its Release, but as for stopping it...an entire coverage of Earth's atmosphere with evaporative dispensing of a neutralizing serum, should prove successful enough to stop it in its tracks." James suddenly begins to feel dizzy. He looks at Burke with sleepy eyes, holding out his glass with a groggy tone and says, "What…drink?" Burke takes James' drink and says, "Night, night son." James passes out on the couch.

   Back on Earth In the dark and now windy desert hills, Debbie and Davis still run from the Tre'toan creature. Closely by, Nelson and Barnes run on top of a cliff's edge towards Davis and Debbie's location. Nelson looking down, sees in the distance brief segments of the Tre'toan creature's movement through the rocks. He suddenly stops, and Barnes stops, both of them panting. Nelson points, "Look! What is that?"
"It sure ain't no firefly, I'll tell ya that!"
"Come on, let's go!"
Nelson and Barnes continue running towards the direction of the creature. Debbie and Davis now exhausted, jogging along with every ounce of energy they can possibly muster. They see the road up ahead of them in the distance. "Look, the road's up ahead," says Davis as he begins to hold his chest, and panting heavily with total perspiration. Right behind them, the creature begins closing in on them. They finally reach the road where the two vehicles still sit unattained. "Hurry…get in," shouts Davis as they pull on the door handles to Nelson's Suburban, but the doors are locked.
"Shit," shouts Davis as he turns to see the creature approaching them. "Come on, get on top of the truck,"

Davis shouts to Debbie as they both quickly climb on to the hood, then over the windshield onto the roof. They look at the front of the Suburban and all around, but can't see the creature anywhere. Suddenly its hissing sound is heard.

"Where is it Chief," asks Debbie as she hides behind him, shaking with fear.

"I don't know." Suddenly one of the rear tires blows out. They look down at the ground by the blown tire, but see nothing, as the other rear tire blows out. Debbie screams briefly with fright and says, "What is it doing?" Davis uses his shoulder radio, "Nelson? Where in the hell are you?" Nelson and Barnes standing with their guns aimed about fifty feet away from the Suburban, and Nelson shouts, "Right here! Get off the truck, now!" Davis and Debbie stand up quickly and jump off the back of the Suburban and hit the ground hard, then get back to their feet, and run like hell as Nelson and Barnes spray the entire side of the Suburban with bullets trying to kill the creature on the side of it. The creature lets out a long and eerie screech as a bullet pierces the gas tank, and the suburban blows up twenty feet skyward into the air, then returning to the ground in a smashing inferno of flames. Davis and Debbie hit the deck, as Nelson and Barnes lower their guns. "Wooo hooo! That critter's toast," Shouts Nelson. Barnes comment's, "I think the Chief's gonna be upset...his ride?"

Davis and Debbie get to their feet and look at the remains of the Suburban, and smoldering blob of Tre'toan flesh. Davis approaches Nelson and Barnes with a serious face and says,

70

"You just wasted taxpayer's money! But well
spent men. Well spent."
Davis holds out his hand for a shake, and Nelson
and Barnes smile and shake hands. Debbie looks
at Davis and asks, "What about my husband
Chief? Where is he?" Davis faces her with a look
of comfort, and holds her shoulders. "Don't worry
Mrs. Lowery. I'm sure he's gonna be all right,
Ok? Where ever he is…I'm sure his thoughts are
with you." Debbie smiles with sorrow and lowers
her head, "Yes, I'm sure they are."

   Back on Silus in Burke's underground laboratory, James
lays restrained on an operation
table again, only in his boxers. A fish net of wires
covers his entire body from the neck down, and
round cylinder probes extrude out of the table and
stop at the sides of his ears. Burke sits at a control
panel pushing buttons and turning knobs. He
signals to Deek standing at a power lever to turn on
the juice. Deek pulls down on the lever and
suddenly a humming noise fills the laboratory. On
the operation table, the fish net wiring begins to
glow bright blue, as electricity current travels along
the probes next to James' ears. James begins to
shake like a fish out of water, and mumbling
repetitively. Burke and Deek remain still during
the DNA extraction process. Suddenly James
opens his eyes and screams briefly, then passes out.

   Moments later, James now lays on the couch in Burke's
living room again…fully dressed, sleeping with his mouth
wide open, and snoring. Burke sitting
across from him is enjoying a Silustrian ale.

James begins to mumble in his sleep, then suddenly wakes up, and sits straight up with a terrifying look while gasping. He feels his head, then his chest while looking at Burke, "Did you…drug me Professor?"

"You appear to be in good health."

"You did."

"No need to worry James…we now have the final ingredients for the serum."

"Easy for you to say. You didn't just have a nightmare from hell!"

"For that, I sincerely apologize. And I can promise you…It doesn't have to happen again." Burke takes a drink then smiles at James. James begins to wear a smile and points his finger at Burke while saying, "Your quite the clever old dog."

"They don't consider me, a cunning Professor for nothing you know."

CHAPTER 8
ELEVATION

Driving down the dark desert road, is the
Tre'toan's SUV. Davis driving, Debbie riding
shotgun, and Nelson and Barnes in the back seat.
"I still don't think it's a good idea to have that
thing in our presence Mrs. Lowery," says Davis as he
briefly looks at Debbie's lap. Debbie holds up the Tre'toan
device concealed in a zip lock bag. Nelson leans forward
and says, "Yeah, that thing could be a bomb or something.
For all we know…more of those things could be looking
for it." Debbie briefly looks at nelson and Davis while
saying, "And that's one reason I'm keeping it. Maybe
somehow or someway it'll bring James back. So don't
thing about taking it away from me…that is if you want to
keep this information from the public."
Davis looks in the rear view at Nelson and Barnes,
"We wouldn't dare think of it Mrs. Lowery…
would we boys?" Nelson and Barnes look at each
other quickly and both answer, "No Sir." Davis
staring forward at the road says, "See Mrs. Lowery, nothing
to worry about." Debbie continues to stare at the device, as
they drive away.

Returning to Burke's home on Silus, James and
Burk stand by the door ready to exit. Burke tugs a
little on the collar of James' jacket while saying,
"You can't go to the Queen's dinner hall looking
like this."
"What's wrong with my duds Professor? Do I not
fit shall we say, the Queen's criteria?" Burke
crosses his arms and says, "No…it's just they, well,
smell poorly." James smells his underarms and
replies," Ok, I can agree with you on that note."

Next we see James and Burke in a Silustrian clothing store…Burke standing with his arms crossed watching James enter a changing room with a stack of clothing. Other Silustrians and Humans present shopping. After a moment, James exits the change room wearing a super tight alien spandex suit, so tight that he can barely breath. He looks at Burke who is about to bust out laughing and says, "Hey, I could get use to this. Ya think my wife would like it?" James walks like a toy wooden soldier back into the change room, and Burke bust's out laughing.

Back on Earth in front of the local Police department, the black SUV pulls up and parks. Everyone including Debbie holding the Tre'toan device, exits the vehicle and walks up the steps into the department. Once inside, Davis says to Debbie, "One moment, I'll be right with ya." Debbie nods as Davis takes Nelson to the side, "I want you to call up Dixie and ask her to come on down. And don't tell her anything yet, Ok?" "Sure Chief." Nelson and Barnes walk away as Davis walks over to Debbie, and gestures her to enter his office. They enter his office and Davis closes the door, then they sit down…Davis sitting behind his desk, and Debbie in front of the desk. Debbie still holding the Tre'toan device in her lap. "I still can't believe it. Murderous Aliens from, Tre'token, or whatever. UFOs snatching up my husband. And they said we're all gonna die some how. What are we gonna do Chief?"
"We just need to relax for a little while first, Ok? I'm sure there's a logical explanation for all of this."

Debbie just looks down at the Tre'toan device and caresses it with her thumb.

"You gonna be alright," asks Davis, as Debbie doesn't reply. "Mrs. Lowery?"

"Yes," says Debbie with a saddened tone. Davis stands up and walks to the door, opens it, then asks Debbie, "Would you care for some coffee or donuts ?" Debbie slowly shakes her head and replies, "Thanks, but no thanks."

"I'll be right back." Davis exits the office, closing the door behind him. "Where are you James?" Says Debbie in her time of sadness, and concerned thoughts for James.

Returning to Silus, in a large hallway leading to Queen Mirla's dinner hall on Silus, several humans, Silustrians and other Alien species walk towards the entrance. James wearing a hefty sized white jumpsuit, Burke wearing a formal gray suit, and Deek as himself walk along together towards the entrance. A faint sound of strange alien rhythmic music gets louder, as they approach the entrance. Also, flashes of light emanating from within the dinner hall. As James, Burke and Deek enter the hall, the music sounds intrinsic, as dozens of Humans and Silustrians dance around the hall in a display of grace and culture. James looks up at the ceiling and to his surprise, sees dozens of multi colored orbs flying all around, and forming various shapes to the beat of the music. James once again in total awe asks Burke, "Are those what I think they are Professor?"

"Yes...the ever so mysterious, and elusive orbs."

"Wow...more truth around every corner."

Mirla dressed in a skin-tight bodysuit, wearing a

jewel fashioned belt and her tiara, walks up to them
while smiling at James...and her gender appearing
to be normal.

"Good evening," she says softly.

James peels his eyes away from the orbs to see
Mirla standing right in front of him, making eyes at
him. James with a surprising look says,

"Oh, hello there your majesty."

"You can call me Mirla."

She instantly takes James by the arm and leads him
into the hall. James looks back at Burke following
them, and gives him an eye-widening plea for help.
Burke trying to contain his laughter, simply shrugs
his shoulders. James then glares at Burke, and turns
his head. After they walk through the choreography
of dancers, James and Mirla come to a series of
floor couches. Mirla forces James to sit next to her
on a couch. James scoots away from her a little, as
she continues to hold his arm, as Burke and Deek sit
down next to them.

   In another remote part of the Universe, is a planet,
Tre'toa, dark in color, and two small suns with no
moons in the distance. A Tre'toan ship suddenly
fly's by toward the planet. On the planet surface, dark low
lying constructed buildings of various proportion outline
the perimeter of a massive, tall structure with large
openings, with red lights shimmering all about
them. The Tre'toan ship approaches one of the
openings at idle speed.

   Inside the structure, the Tre'toan ship lands inside
a triangular docking port, surrounded by dozens of
other ships docked. Deep inside the structure, the

Lord Zemious, leader of the evil Tre'toan, dressed
in a deep red hooded cloak, wearing large chrome
inscribed bracelet's sits on a dark granite throne...in
a large chamber constructed of a dark composite
type steel, with one large octagon light located in
the center of the ceiling. Two Tre'toan guards
dressed in gloss black uniforms similar to military
issue, stand on each side of Zemious, and hold in
their hands chrome laser rifles. A Tre'toan soldier
also in a gloss black uniform enters and takes a knee
before Zemious.
"My Lord Zemious, I regret to inform you of a
change in events on our mission to Earth."
Zemious removes his hood quickly, and he appears
to look mid-aged.
"Change in events," Zemious asks with an already angered
tone.
"The Silustrians my Lord. Again, they have
interrupted our plans to fore go the elimination of
the Earthlings." Zemious stands quickly as his eyes glow
with fire. "The virus, released it you have?"
"Yes my Lord...but." Zemious interrupts,
"But what?"
"We failed to retrieve the Human specimen. The
Silustrians managed to grab him before we could."
Zemious' eyes suddenly shoot fire at the soldier, the
soldier shrieking and burning to a cinder. Zemious'
eyes return to their normal state, as the soldier's
corpse smolders.
"Fetch me the fleet commander, now," Zemious shouts as
the two guards jog away. Zemious squints as he says,
"Now...the long awaited war of wars will begin." His eyes
briefly flash with fire.

CHAPTER 9
INVASION

The light of day now pierces through the blinds
of Davis' office windows, as Debbie sleeps in the
chair, still grasping the Tre'toan device. Davis can
be seen through his interior office window talking
to Nelson and Barnes. They finish talking, then
Nelson and Barnes walk away, as Dixie
approaches Davis. They talk for a moment, then
Davis points at Debbie. Dixie nods her head and
walks to the door, opening and entering the office.
Dixie places her hands ever so gently on Debbie's
shoulders. Debbie suddenly wakes up shouting,
"James! James!"
"It's Ok mam. Your safe," says Dixie as
Debbie looks at Dixie with sadness. Dixie hugs
her and softly says, "Oh you poor dear."
After a moment of Dixie's comforting Debbie, they draw
away from the hugging and Debbie has tears in her eyes
slowly running down her cheeks. Dixie takes out a tissue
and wipes her tears away while saying, "There there…it's
gonna be alright. Dixie's here to take care of ya honey."
Debbie begins to show a little smile. "That's more like it."
Dixie stands up and extends her hand to Debbie.
"Come on. You can stay with me, Ok?" Debbie
nods and replies, "Ok", as she takes Dixie's hand
and stands up. They both turn and exit the office.

At Queen Mirla's dinner hall on Silus, everyone has left
but Deek who lays asleep on the couch with his
legs stretched out over Burke's lap. Burke passed
out with an empty bottle in one hand, and in the
other an empty glass…while James barely sits up
drunk and singing, as Mirla is wide awake and
slightly clinging on James' arm. James singing,

"God bless America…my home sweet," James suddenly passes out on to the couch. Mirla shakes her head and stands up. She then leans over and amazingly picks up James in her arms with ease, then walks away with him.

In Mirla's chambers, a large round bed with several exotic pillows, and fine silky curtains hang from the ceiling all around. She enters with James in her arms and proceeds to the bed. She then gently lays James on the bed. He rolls over and hugs a pillow. She then turns and walks away.

Back in the evil Lord Zemious' lair on Tre'toa, he paces slowly around another soldier. "A surprise attack from our entire fleet, shall put an end to their further interference with our goals. What else of further use do you recommend commander?"
"Perhaps a campaign of fusion missile bombardment, to severely fracture they're Capital City installations… rendering their main communications weak."
Zemious stops and faces the commander.
"Yes…a brilliant idea. Assemble the fleet and all the missiles we can possibly carry. We'll give them such a war…they'll fear our very existence. And the moment victory is near…invade them we will. This moment has gone unanswered far too long. See to it Commander."
"Yes my Lord."
The commander bows briefly and walks away.
Zemious wears an evil grin.

Returning to Queen Mirla's chambers on Silus, James now lays under the covers still fully

dressed, and Mirla lays under the covers in a
skimpy nightgown, on the opposite side of the bed.
Both of them sleeping. James rolls over towards
Mirla, and his hand touches Mirla's shoulder.
James dreaming of Debbie and him rolling around
in bed. James now lightly caressing Mirla's
shoulder. She smiles and moans a little. James
still dreaming of Debbie's face in the heat of
passion. Now James kissing Mirla's shoulder…
Mirla moans a little and rolls over towards James.
James suddenly opens his eyes and they widen to
the extreme. He screams and Mirla opens her eyes
as James jumps up and rolls out of bed hitting the
floor hard. "Owwww," he shouts.
Mirla pulls herself to the side of the bed to see
James sitting up rubbing his head. She laughs
briefly, and James suddenly looks at her again
with the widest eyes, and shakes is hand briefly in
her face. "Stay there," says James as he quickly
gets to his feet and adds, "Your Majesty…
goodnight." James walks away quickly while shaking his
head as Mirla rests her head on her hands and says, "Why
is it always the cute ones?"

  Back home on Earth in Dixie's house, Dixie sits
on the bed next to Debbie lying down under the
covers. "You rest as long as you need to, Ok?"
Debbie nods and replies, "Thank you."
"Don't mention it Honey. I'll be home later on."
They both smile as Dixie stands up and walks
away. Debbie pulls out the Tre'toan device and
looks at it, as she dozes off. Debbie now holding the device
in the palm of her hand, the device begins to open up, until
fully opened. The strange refractive

82

letters and shapes begin to rise up into the air. Debbie
begins to dream of the evil Tre'toan's plans to eliminate the
entire inhabitance of Earth's population…People choking
and dying at homes, in cars, office buildings and City
streets…by the millions.
The Tre'toan device slips out of her hands and
falls onto the floor, shattering into pieces. Debbie
still dreaming, as tears run down her cheeks.

   Looking at the exterior of Lord Zemious'
towering complex of darkness on Tre'toa, Zemious stands
at the entrance of a landing bay, watching the
Tre'toan fleet vessels exiting dozens of bays by the
dozens. He briefly throws up his hands to them,
turns and walks towards an enormous ship
awaiting his presence aboard. Next, the huge
command ship exits the bay and fly's skyward
towards the Tre'toan fleet.

   In Burke's house on Silus, the front door opens,
and James helps Burke into the house who is still
drunk , and Deek staggering a little enters as well.
James helps Burke to one of the couches, and
Burke falls onto the couch and quickly dozes off.
"The doctor has left the building," says James as
he falls backwards onto one of the couches. Deek
staggers up to the center table, drops to his knees
and passes out face first onto the table. James
looking up at the ceiling closes his eyes, when
suddenly a super loud fart sounds throughout the
house. James sits up quickly with a disgusted look,
and notices Deek smiling.
"I've the perfect house warming gift for you…a
cork!" James quickly lays back down face first into a

83

couch cushion.

Light years away Aboard the Command Bridge of
Zemious' ship, he sits on a throne type chair accompanied
by his personal guards, and about ten crewmen controlling
the ship. He presses a lighted symbol on his armrest. "How
long Commander, before we can make the jump?"
In a lower section of the ship, the Commander
standing at a voice console on the wall replies,"
"Just a short while longer my Lord."
The Commander then turns to view dozens of
crewmen loading dozens of slender liquid filled
missiles into missile batteries located in the deck
of the ship. Back on Zemious' bridge, he says
aloud to a crewman in front of him at a console,
"Alert the fleet of our readiness for light-speed!"
"Yes my Lord."
In space, the entire Tre'toan fleet of at least a
hundred or so vessels, fly's by and away, with
Zemious' ship bringing up the rear.

Back home In Olsen's office, he sits back in his
chair, smoking a cigar while on the phone. He
speaks harshly on the phone.
"No, I don't know where his wife is either! And
I don't need you TV buffs nosing around here as
well! Good day!" Olsen slams down the phone, stands up
quickly and storms out of his office and demands loudly,
"Anyone seen, or heard from Lowery?"
Everyone present working shakes their heads no.
A moment goes by and Olsen shouts,
"What are yea staring at! Get back to work!"
Everybody quickly gets busy as Olsen re-enters his

office, slamming the door behind him and
shouting, "Damn that Lowery! He's finished!"

  Back in Dixie's house, Debbie with wet hair in
just a towel is talking on the phone in Dixie's
kitchen, "I appreciate you filling in for me Laura. I just
need a little time to sort some things out. Thanks
Laura, goodbye." She hangs up and sits at the kitchen table
in front of her. She sips a cup of coffee, then suddenly set's
it down and picks up a newspaper. The
paper reads: Unidentified virus claims forty-three
lives in South America. After a moment of reading
the newspaper, She slowly sets down the paper as
she lifts her head and thinks to herself.

  Nine light years from Earth, Zemious and his
dark fleet prepare to jump to light speed. All the
ships assume a divided formation on each side of
Zemious' Ship. On Zemious' bridge, Zemious gives the
order to jump to light speed. "Ready commander!"
The Commander walks up to a seat just below
Zemious, and sits while saying towards the crewmen at the
flight control console, "All ships to engage on my mark!"
Watching the ships from behind their location, all of the
ships starting from the ones most forward, jump to light
speed, gone in a fraction of a second.

  In the dark stillness of night on Silus, the Capital
City Streets lay empty of any signs of life. Only
the strangely shaped lights that adorn the
buildings, provide any light what so ever.
Suddenly the deep and loud sound of pulsating
Sirens fill the entire city with the fearful warning

of the incoming threat of the Tre'toans arrival. Dozens of Silustrian UFO crewmen exit several buildings, running in one direction, towards the UFO landing ports. Dozens of more Silustrians dressed in dark blue battle gear, holding slender chrome laser guns and rifles, also exit buildings. Humans and Silustrians also exit quickly from their dwellings, curious of the alarm and actions of the crewmen and soldiers.

In Burke's house, James, Burke and Deek all suddenly wake up. Burke and Deek run to the door, it opens quickly, and they step outside. James sits up and says, "What's all the fuss about?"

On Zemious' bridge, him and the entire crew can see the Capital City through their bridge windows. "Move the fleet into flank position and fire your missiles Commander!"
The Commander briefly bows to Zemious and faces the crew captain sitting in a revolving chair and orders, "Signal the fleet and begin missile bombardment!" The Captain swivels to his control panel. Looking at the Tre'toan ships, the fleet ships fly down over the City in a V formation, as Zemious' ship flies forward towards the City.

Burke and Deek still standing outside of the doorway, watching all the Silustrian and Human civilians frantically running around and screaming, as the Tre'toans quickly descend on the City, and begin firing their lasers and fusion missiles all over. The Silustrian soldiers begin firing back at the Tre'toan ships, as Tre'toan lasers hit buildings and civilians, and missiles exploding all over in liquid embers, instantly dissolving their targets. Burke runs back into his house and towards the lab entrance behind the bar. "Don't move James," shouts Burke, as he runs down into the Lab. With the sound of the events taking place just outside and watching Burke, James stands up and runs over to the door.

At the UFO landing port, the Silustrian fleet quickly board their ships. One of the UFOs is suddenly fired upon heavily and explodes, sending debris everywhere, as the UFOs begin to take off. Laser cannons pop up atop the Cities buildings and begin firing at the Tre'toan ships. James leaning on the doorway looking out at the battle, sees Mirla running down a corridor in fear for her life. A fusion missile hits one of the columns supporting the roof of the corridor, dissolving the lower portion, and causing the roof to collapse just in front of her. James quickly looks at Deek and says, "I'm gonna help her!" James runs to Mirla's rescue.

Above the City, Silustrian UFOs battling Tre'toan UFOs. Aboard Zemious' bridge, Zemious remains in his chair, While the Commander stands and says aloud to the Captain, "Prepare the second approach of missile bombardment!" The Captain nods and turns to his console.

Back to the battle scene in the streets of the

Capital City, James dodging laser fire runs his
Fastest to reach the Queen's location. Just about to
her, a laser hits the ground next to his feet, igniting
his boots on fire, as he screams and dives over the
rubble pile from the corridor. He land's next to
Mirla who is ok and kneeling down behind the
rubble. James quickly begins stomping his feet and
blowing on them hard to put out the flames. James
decides to pull off his boots quickly. Burke jogs
up and out of the lab carrying a medium size
chrome briefcase, and two laser pistols. He runs
out the door and stops facing Deek while gasping.
"Where's James?"
Deek points to James and Mirla's location while
replying, "There, to save the Queen."
Burke hands Deek a laser pistol.
"Take this…follow me!"
Burke runs towards James and Mirla, and Deek
follows hot on his heels.

  Above the City, Zemious' ship flies above
making another run with the fusion missiles, as the
UFOs continue their fighting.

  In a remote area a hundred miles away from
the Silustrian Capital City, on the dark horizon
some five miles away, little specks of bright
lights moving in various patterns, become larger
by the second. After a moment it becomes clear
the lights are orbs, traveling hundreds of miles per
hour. They pass and fly away quickly towards the
Capital City.

  Burke and Deek reach James and Mirla, both

hiding behind the rubble. James putting on his now soaking wet boots. "Are you all right your Highness," asks Burke.

"Yes, I'm fine."

Burke then sniffs the air and asks, "What is that smell?" James finishing with his boots replies, "Don't ask." A brief moment later, James adds, "I guess the Tre'toans found out about our little secret."

"Yes, it would appear so," says Burke as the battling from all directions continues.

Inside the Police station, Dixie sitting back in a chair and reading a book. The phone rings and Dixie pushes a button on the switchboard.

"Hello?" A brief moment goes by.

"Oh, hey girl. How ya doing?"

In Dixie's kitchen, Debbie on the phone.

"Alright. Say Dixie, is the Chief available?"

Dixie's voice answers, "Sure, hang on a minute, I'll fetch him."

"Thanks."

In the station, Dixie stands up and walks over to Davis's door, opens it and leans into see Davis holding up a mirror, looking at his bald head.

"Chief?" Davis suddenly hides the mirror while looking at Dixie. "What ever happened to knocking?" Replies Davis, as Dixie wears a smile.

"Mrs. Lowery's on line two."

"Here we go." Says Davis, as Dixie still smiling closes the door and walks away. Davis picks up the phone. "Hello Mrs. Lowery, is everything alright?"

Debbie on the phone in Dixie's kitchen. "I don't

think so Chief. It's already started." Davis's asks,
"What's all ready started?"
"The alien's plans to kill us off. It's started
already in South America, a virus…an unknown
virus… growing and killing people." Davis on the
phone, "And how do you know what your
saying's true?"
Debbie on the phone, "It's right on the front page
of the Chronicle. Don't you read the paper?"
Davis on the phone, "Not really. Look Mrs.
Lowery…we don't need to jump to any
conclusions here. There's always diseases, killing
people all the time. So what makes this one any
different from all the rest?"
Debbie on the phone with a serious look,
"And what if I'm right, and we all die because
we didn't do anything about it? Don't you care
about that possibility Chief?"
Davis on the phone, "Well of course I would,"
It's just that I don't see", Davis here's the phone
click. "Mrs. Lowery?" After no reply, Davis
sighs and hangs up the phone, then leans back in
his chair thinking to himself.

   Returning to the battle in the Capital City on
Silus, James, Burke , Deek and Mirla still seek
shelter behind The pile of rubble, as the laser fire
from the war continues to pose a threat to anyone
caught in its crossfire. "We've gotta get you out of here
James, and back to Earth with the Serum."
   "I couldn't agree with you more," replies James as they see
Zemious' ship flying overhead, firing missiles and laser
shots forward and ahead of their position.
Burke peeks out from behind the rubble and

notices the fighting has decreased near their own position. He looks at James and Mirla, "Alright, this it. Follow my lead, and stay close as you can." James nods as Burke peeks one more time, then rises to his feet and runs away with everyone closely following behind him.

Approximately a half a mile away from the cities outskirts, the orbs in the distance spread out and fly in all directions. A Tre'toan ship giving chase to a Silustrian ship, is chased itself suddenly by two of the orbs.
Aboard the Tre'toan ship's bridge, a crewman scanning an octagon shaped radar screen sees the orbs presence behind them and quickly turns to his Captain and shouts, "Energy mites approaching!" Suddenly orbs enter the Ship's Bridge and the Captain and crew tense up as orbs penetrate the ship' s control consoles, creating massive sparks, intense explosions and panic for the entire crew.
Just outside of the ship, the orbs quickly exit it and fly away, as the ship begins to blow up and disintegrate.

Still continuing their trek, Burke, James, Deek and Mirla run into a long one-story building. Once inside they see a couple of Silustrian soldiers, walking towards them, one helping the other due to injury. Everyone quickly jogs up to them and they all stop, then one of the soldiers says,
"Penetrated the compound they have."
"How many," asks Burke.
"Don't know. Turn back you must."

"I think we'd better take their advice and turn back Professor, don't you," asks James as suddenly laser fire barely wings the wounded soldier's back, sending him to the floor, and everyone else ducking. Half a dozen Tre'toan foot soldiers run towards them, firing their weapons as they approach. James quickly bends over and picks up the injured soldier, and holds him over his shoulder and runs away with everyone else running away as well.

On the bridge of a Silustrian UFO, the crew witnesses through their bridge window, their orb friends penetrating the Tre'toan ships and destroying them. The crew smiling and cheering for the moment. From a distance above the city up in the sky, the orbs can be seen flying everywhere, attributing to the many explosions all over the sky from the disintegrating Tre'toan ships.
On Zemious' control bridge, the Captain quickly turns toward Zemious and the Commander, "We've lost communications with most of the fleet!" Zemious' eyes begin to glow red as he quickly stands and says with anger, "How can that be! A view of the remaining ships, now!"
Another crewman pushes a button and a hologram appears, showing several of the Tre'toan ships being invaded by the orbs, and being destroyed. The Captain says, "Energy mites my Lord!" Zemious responds fiercely, "Who is responsible for this lack of information?"
Zemious looks at the Commander, then the Captain, and the Captain looking at Zemious briefly glances at the Commander. Zemious' eyes

begin to burn with fire as he looks at the
Commander. The Commander suddenly takes a
knee and pleads with Zemious, "Please my Lord…I swear I
did not know of their presence upon our arrival." Two fire
beams suddenly exit Zemious' eyes and hit the
Commander's, blowing him back against
the bridge wall in a brief fireball…the remains of
the Commander but a smoldering shell. Zemious
sits down and looks at the entire crew whom all
bow briefly from their fear of the moment.
"Recall the remaining ships and troops
Captain…and set a holding pattern away from the
planet!"
"Yes my Lord." The Captain bows briefly and turns to his
console. "They'll pay fiercely for this," says Zemious with
determination.

CHAPTER 10
ANNHILATION

In Dixie's living room, Debbie now dried off and
fully dressed in a pair of jeans and a T-shirt, sits
down on the couch in front of the television and
uses the remote. The television comes on and
Debbie flips through a couple of channels and
stops on her news channel. Her co-anchor Bob
Spencer telling the news, "With the death toll now rising to
approximately one hundred and seventy three, all airports,
trains, bus lines and shipping of any kind, have been
suspended in South America, due to the sudden and
increasing risk of the still unidentified virus. Their
government forces have quarantined a four hundred square
mile perimeter, in hopes of
stopping the virus from possibly spreading any
further. In other news, the stock market," Debbie
turns off the television and leaves the couch. She
walks into the kitchen and uses the phone. She
dials a number. "Yes, I need a cab please."
Debbie now at the front door, opens it and exits
the house. On the kitchen table she has left a
thank you note for Dixie.

At the police department in Davis's office, he sits
in his chair and leans forward, then uses the phone.
After a moment of no reply, he gets up and walks
quickly out of his office.

Back in the compound on Silus, our friend's run
and take shelter around a corner from the intense
laser fire from the Tre'toan foot soldiers. Our
friends now being trapped at a dead end. Burke
and Deek exchanging laser fire, as everyone else
stays low and close to the wall. "I don't know
how much longer we can hold them off," shouts

Burke while firing his gun. James looking all around for a way out of their situation. He notices a square outline on the floor. He faces the soldier and points at it, "Where does that lead to?" "Vast subterranean cavities…lead to port terminals they do." James quickly gets to his knees and tries to open the hatch with his bare fingers, but can't. He turns to Mirla?

"Might I borrow your belt Mirla?"

She smiles and replies, "Certainly." She unbuckles it and hands it to James. Burke and Deek still firing at the Tre'toan soldiers. One of the Tre'toan soldiers ducked down and holding a small gold octagon shaped disk in his hand, speaks into it, "We have the Queen and her conspirators sieged! Requesting more troops!"

On Zemious' bridge, he sits in his chair listening to the soldier's request. Zemious replies, "We cannot afford to lose any more ships! Order them to continue, and if the Queen and her conspirators resist…kill them all!" An octagon shaped radar scope displays several incoming Silustrian UFOs. The crewman at the scope turns quickly to Zemious, "Silustrian vessels approaching from our port side my Lord!" In space at a distance of approximately one kilometer, the Silustrian ships close in quickly for a counter attack against the Tre'toans. Ships from both sides engaging each other with massive laser fire exchange.

Returning to the inside of the compound on Silus, James now with the lid off the shaft, hands

Mirla her belt and crawls down onto a ladder attached to the shaft wall. He looks at Burke and Deek who are still firing at the Tre'toans, and shouts, "Professor! Come on!"
"I'll provide us enough time to get everyone out...go," shouts Burke. James gestures the seriously wounded soldier to get on his back. "Don't worry, I won't drop ya. Just hang on tight." Mirla and the other soldier help him on to James' back. The soldier wraps his arms around James' neck too tightly, and James begins to choke, then trying to speak but can't. He suddenly loses his footing, and slides down the ladder with the soldier...both yelling all the way down. James finally tightening his grip good, and using his boots to slow them down...coming to a complete stop and James still yelling briefly. James' boots just inches from the floor of a narrow tunnel carved out of the Earth, and dimly lit by small flat and circular overhead lights. He helps the soldier off his back and assists him to the ground against the wall out of harms-way. Mirla looking down at them shouts, "Are you Ok down there?" James looks up and shouts back, "We're still alive, if that's what you mean!"

Near the outskirts on the opposite side of the city, several Silustrian soldiers tucked tightly behind an enormous statue that resembles an Alien Sun God, exchange laser fire with Tre'toan foot soldiers. Suddenly in the near distance, two dozen or more orbs approach rapidly, and assume a position over the Tre'toan foot soldiers location. They suddenly descend on them, in a spiraling and fast motion…entering them as the soldiers begin to shriek, then blowing them into pieces as the Silustrian soldiers jump up and cheer with their hands held high in celebration. After the orbs finish destroying the remaining Tre'toans…they form an alien's face that smiles.

   As Burke and Deek exchange laser fire with the Tre'toans, Deek shoots and hits one of them in the chest, blowing him back several feet…and the Tre'toan shrieks to his death. A creature instantly exits, but only half way out, it screeches its last breath…falling to the ground with its tongue hanging out dead. Mirla and the other Silustrian soldier carefully enter the shaft and proceed downward, as Burke hands the briefcase to Deek, "Go Deek…go now!"
"But Professor." Burke interrupts,
"Trust me, I'll be just fine…now go!"
Deek takes one last shot, then runs over to the shaft and enters it, climbing downward quickly.

   Back on Earth in front of James and Debbie's house, a cab pulls into the driveway. Debbie exits from the rear left passenger side, closes the door quickly and hands the cabby a twenty, then turns and proceeds to the front door as the cabby backs out and pulls away. At the front door, Debbie places her hand on the knob and twists, but the door doesn't open. She puts her shoulder into it and the door jam breaks off while it opens. She looks closely at the jam…and it reveals globs of chewing gum.
"Gum," Debbie questions as she enters the house.

At Dixie's house, Davis driving a Police cruiser, and Dixie riding shotgun pull into the driveway quickly and park. Davis and Dixie exit the car quickly with their guns drawn…Dixie behind Davis. They make their way quickly to the front door and stop. Davis looks at Dixie and nods, then opens the door quickly…running into the house with their guns aimed.

"Mrs. Lowery," shouts Davis, as they both cautiously spread out… Dixie towards the kitchen area, and Davis towards the bedrooms.

"Are you here Mrs. Lowery?" Still with no reply, Davis approaches the guest room where Debbie slept, and opens the door quickly with his gun drawn in front of him. He notices the broken pieces of the Tre'toan device on the floor. He starts to walk towards them and they suddenly burst into red-hot lava…and after a moment turn cold and explode into a powder sort of ash. Davis jumps back and almost falls backwards. His face full of curiosity as he regains his composure… looking at the mysterious dust cloud engulfing the entire room. He holsters his gun and walks back to the living room, where Dixie stands holding the brief note left by Debbie on the kitchen table. Davis stops in front of Dixie and takes the note and looks at it. It reads: Thank you Dixie, love Debbie.

"What was that noise back there Chief," asks Dixie. "Just another clue that Mrs. Lowery isn't here," replies Davis as he walks to the front door, then turns to Dixie, "Come on, I need you back at the station." Davis turns and walks out the door, and Dixie asks while following him Outside the house,

99

"You wanna tell me what's really going on here Chief?"
Davis hesitates to answer her, as he opens his car door.
Dixie walking over to her door asks, "Well?"
"Trust me when I tell you…that the less you
know…the better off you'll be." Davis gets in the
car, shuts the door and starts the engine, as Dixie
opens her door and enters the car. She asks him
one more question, "So where do you suppose she
went?" Davis backs out, then pulls away and
replies, " Not far...I'll find her."

  Returning to the battle in space over Silus, the
full scale battle continues…Silustrian ships
chasing Tre'toan ships, and visa versa…as large
cannons on Zemious' ship fire at several Silustrian
ships trying to get in closer for a more effective
hit. One of Zemious' cannons fires repetitively on
a Silustrian ship, blowing it to pieces.
On Zemious' control bridge, he remains seated
and calm for the moment, as the massive battling
is seen through the bridge window. The Captain
turns to Zemious, "They're attempting to take out our Aft
Thruster systems!"
"I trust you'll handle the situation without failure Captain?"
"Yes my Lord."
The Captain turns to his console and speaks,
"All ships draw their fire away from our Aft
position!" In all directions around Zemious' ship the
fighting continues…ships from both sides being destroyed.

  Returning to our friends on Silus, Burke still

firing at the Tre'toan soldiers, hits one dead center
in the gut, blowing him back several feet. The
soldier screeches to his death. Burke decides it's a
good time to flee the scene, so he runs to the shaft
while tucking his laser pistol down his pants,
climbs into the shaft and straddles the ladder,
then slides quickly all the way down to the bottom.
At the bottom, everyone looking at Burke and
James asks, "What took you so long?"
Burke grins while replying, "Target practice…let's go."
James once more helps the wounded soldier onto
his back, and everyone jogs away down the long
and narrow cavity. Just above the shaft, the four
remaining Tre'toan foot soldiers stop, and one of
them pulls a dark round sphere off his belt clip and
says, "This will slow them down."
He presses a button inward, then drops it down the
shaft. At the bottom of the shaft, the dark sphere
now having four red laser sights stops three feet
from impacting the floor. Suddenly four little
laser barrels pop out as it begins to make a distinct
humming noise, like the sound of a powerful
transformer. It begins to move in on our friend's
direction. Our friends still jogging along and
Burke suddenly slows down. The seeking sphere
continues to move faster and faster. Burke stops
in his tracks, and everyone else as well. They turn
and look at him. "What is it Professor,"
asks James. "Shhh," replies Burke with his
finger up. The seeking sphere still moving fastly
towards them, as Burke speaks quickly,
"Everyone down on the ground, now!"
Burke and everyone quickly lay down, including
the wounded soldier still on James' back.

101

"Don't move a muscle…or breathe heavy for that matter," whispers Burke. The seeking sphere now moving slower and slower arrives at their location, probing the entire area for any movement with its infrared sights. Everyone with fear in their eyes, watches the sphere as it begins to hover over them, turning and searching for them.

Suddenly a green bug that resembles a small crab with suction cup antennas, crawls out from a crack in the floor and towards Mirla's face. Her eyes widen as she wears the most terrifying look. Only James, the wounded soldier on his back, and the other soldier sees the bug approaching Mirla's face. The seeking sphere slowly moves beyond their position, as the soldier looks at the other soldier on James' back, then Mirla and whispers, "For your honor my Majesty."

The soldier suddenly gets to his feet and runs as quickly as he can back towards the access shaft. The seeking sphere turns quickly and pursues the soldier…speeding over everyone and firing bright but thin lasers at the soldier. The soldier on James' back shouts, "Sim, no!" Burke and Deek begin firing at the sphere, but having a hard time hitting it. Sim now some thirty feet away takes a direct hit to the back, the laser beam cutting clean through him…he falls to the ground and dies. Burke and Deek finally hitting the sphere, and the sphere explodes with the power of a stick of dynamite… and the entire tunnel begins to shake with the area of the spheres destruction, collapsing in. Everyone quickly gets up and runs away as the tunnel caves in behind them…and the alien bug squashed in the process. The soldier on James' back with tears in his eyes sadly says, "Sim," as they continue to run away.

Back home on Earth in front of the Police Station, Davis walks out with Nelson and Barnes following him. "We've gotta find her before anything else can go wrong." Davis stops by his car door, opens it and turns while resting his hands on the door, as Nelson and Barnes stop in front of the black SUV facing Davis. "You boys follow me...but not too closely."
Davis gets in his car and shuts the door, starting his car and backing out, as Nelson and Barnes get in the SUV. Davis peels away.

In front of James and Debbie's house, Debbie exits the front door wearing a white halter-top, and matching overalls...and she carries a little black purse. She closes the front door and walks over to the garage then takes a remote for the garage out of her purse, aims it at the door and presses. The door opens all the way up, revealing a brand new top of the line midnight blue SUV. Debbie gets in, starts it up, then backs out as the garage door closes. Backed up all the way out of the drive, she peels away. Davis and posse pull up to Debbie's and park, just missing her.

Debbie in her SUV driving down the road, places a picture of James and her posing together at an Amusement Park on the center console. In the back ground of the photo, a man maid UFO sits perched on a wide pole. Debbie looking at the photo smiles out of sadness, as a single tear rolls down her cheek.

103

Returning to space over Silus, the battle yet remains in full swing. Aboard one of the Silustrian ships, a crew of six stands at their controls…as the blue containment beams shine down on them from above. One of the crew in the gunnery station, firing and speaking quickly to himself in Silustrian dialect. On his hologram, a Tre'toan ship in his sights. He fires with precision aim and blows it up. He cheers loudly, "Yahaaa!"

Returning to our friends in the long tunnel, they approach another ladder leading upwards and stop. James panting heavier than everyone else, decides to take a short breather, setting the wounded soldier down against the wall.
"If I'm not mistaken, this should lead up to the landing port terminals," says Burke while looking up. Mirla comforts the wounded soldier, as James, Burke, and Deek watch them talking.
"My brother not die in vein your Majesty. Fool was he, but brave as well."
Mirla gently holds his face and replies, "Yes, he shall be honored in the halls of Rue Silus." She softly kisses his forehead, and he smiles a little. Mirla looks at everyone watching. Burke places his hands on the ladder and says, "Sorry folks…but we must be moving on." Burke starts up the ladder as James sighs heavily then helps the wounded and heart broken soldier onto his back again. James and the soldier start up the ladder behind Burke, then Mirla, and Deek left to bring up the rear.

In a room dimly lit by sconce lighting, with silver crates stacked on one another, and two doors located opposite of each other, a floor hatch slowly opens up and it's Burke's face peeking to see if the coast is clear to exit. Seeing that it is, he quickly lifts the hatch lid all the way back and softly lays it down. He then climbs out and helps with James and the soldier first. James panting again says, "Is this the last flight?"

Burke helps him and the soldier all the way out and replies, "We'll know that as soon as we reach the landing port." Burke continues to help Mirla, then Deek. Finished, Burke steps up to one of the doors, where a lighted button on the wall blinks continuously. Burke signals Deek to stand on the opposite side of the door. Deek does so, while they both hold their guns aimed, Burke nods to Deek, then pushes the lighted button, and the door opens upwards swiftly, revealing a long hallway with many openings. Parts of the ceiling and walls appear to have been hit with Zemious' fusion missiles…hundred square foot areas completely gone, and portions of the flooring dissolved. Burke thinking the coast is clear, steps out a few feet and suddenly laser fire from three different guns hits the door jam next to him, as he quickly runs back into the room and seeks shelter behind the wall. "Blasted! They must have been tracking us the whole time," loudly says Burke, as everyone also assumes shelter along the wall. James looking at Burke says, "From the looks of things…I'd say we're right back where we started."

The laser fire suddenly stops and a Tre'toan's voice shouts, "Give us the Queen, and we'll spare the rest of you! And if you refuse, you all will be annihilated! You have but a few moments to decide!" Burke looks at the chrome crates and notices a particular symbol on its side, resembling an atom. "I've an idea," says Burke.

Back on earth in front of James and Debbie's house, Davis, Nelson and Barnes approach their vehicles and stop. Davis takes off his baseball cap, takes out a rag from his back pocket and wipes his sweaty bald head while saying, "You two go ahead and resume your patrol. If I need your assistance later for any reason, I'll contact yea's." Nelson and Barnes Nod and say, "Yes Sir," as they open their doors. Davis already turned with his cap back on, turns to them again and points his finger while saying aloud, "And remember…you know nothing when it comes to you know what!" They respond with a nod, then get in the SUV, start it up and pull away past Davis. They all wave briefly as Davis gets in his car. He shuts the door and rests his arms on the steering wheel…wondering where Debbie could be. After a moment, he starts his car and pulls away.

Debbie driving down the road, she pulls into Max's gas station, up to the pumps and shuts off the engine. She gets out and is greeted by Max. "Hello there Mrs. Lowery. What can I do ya fur?" Debbie replies, "Hi Max. You can fill it up." "Will do."
Debbie walks towards the store entrance, as Max fills her tank. Davis pulls into the station and to the pumps on the opposite side of Debbie's SUV. He gets out and shuts the door, then walks around

the pumps past Max, towards the store entrance.
"Hey Chief! Filler up,"
says Max aloud. Davis replies aloud,
"You got it!"
"Alrighty", says Max has he begins to fill up
Davis's tank as well. In the store, Davis walks in
and a young man, Tommy, Caucasian, nineteen or
so years old greets Davis, "Hi Chief."
Debbie nowhere in sight, as Davis stops at the
magazine rack and replies,
"Staying out of trouble these days Tommy?"
Davis picks out a magazine and opens it, while
Tommy replies, "Oh yeah…my days of partying
are over."
"That's good to hear Tommy."
Davis places the magazine back and walks toward
the restrooms. Once there, he opens the door and
enters, and at the same time, Debbie exits the
ladies restroom and walks up to the counter.
"That'll be thirty five twenty nine mam,"
says Tommy as Debbie hands him fifty. He works
the register and gives her the change and a receipt.
"Thank You," says Debbie as she walks away
out of the store.
"You're Welcome!"
Outside at the pumps, Debbie gets in her SUV
and Max says aloud, "Bye Mrs. Lowery!"
"Bye Max!"
Debbie shuts the door and starts the engine, then
pulls away. Inside the store in front of the men's restroom
door, the sound of the toilet flushing. A brief
moment later, Davis exits and walks up to the
register. "How much ," asks Davis.
"Twenty five even Sir," replies Tommy.

Davis hands him twenty-five even, then walks towards, and out the door.

"Keep up the good work Tommy!"

Returning to the battle in space above Silus, only a few ships from each fleet remain in the survival of the fittest…still fighting it out, away from, and around Zemious' ship.

On board Zemious' bridge, he gives an order to the Captain, "Speed us up Captain, and set a safer course in orbit over the Capitol!"

The Captain turns to Zemious,

"But my Lord, our remaining ships." Zemious eyes briefly flicker of fire as he interrupts, "Do not question my authority Captain…ever!"

"Forgive me my Lord."

The Captain bows briefly and adds, "As you wish." He turns to his console.

Viewing Zemious' ship in space, it quickly fly's away from the now diminishing battle.

Back on Silus in the storage room, where our friends plot to rid themselves of the Tre'toan foot soldiers, Burke holds what looks like a small nuclear bomb, with one handle on its upper end. A Tre'toan's voice shouts, "Your time is over! Give us the Queen…or you all die!" Burke shout's back, "Just a moment…we're getting her prepared!"

"You have twenty seconds!"

Burke hands the device to James, and he carefully takes it while asking,

"Is this thing nuclear Professor?"

"Heavens no…it's just an atomic switch."

James' eyes widen as he says,
"Just, atomic?"
"Now remember...throw it high in their direction. Got it,"
says Burke. James replies, "Got it."
Burke turns to see Mirla still standing against the
wall, the soldier sitting against the wall, and Deek
standing in an empty chrome crate, with an
attached lid that stands open like a jewelry box.
Deek holding a laser pistol. Burke looks at Deek
and says, "You sure about this Deek?"
"Sure I am."
"Alright." The Tre'toan's voice shouts, "The Queen!
Now!"
"Here she comes," shouts Burke, as James
assumes his position, and Deek squats down in the
crate. Burke assumes a position behind the crate
with his laser pistol in one hand, closes the lid over
Deek, then leans on the crate while saying,
"One Deek in the box, coming right up."
Burke pushes with all his might on the crate, and
releases it just at the doorway...the crate sliding
across the floor some twenty-five feet to a dead
stop, as laser fire sprays the crate, but doing no
damage what so ever. Seeing the direction of the
laser fire, James tosses the device high and far, as
Burke fires at it just before impact, blowing it up,
into an explosion so powerful, the entire complex
shakes, as debris fly's everywhere, and the sound
of Tre'toans shrieking to their deaths.
Suddenly Deek pops up with his laser pistol, just
as the last Tre'toan comes hobbling out and
shooting his laser rifle. Deek fires several rounds
into the Tre'toan soldier killing him. Burke leans
over and picks up the chrome briefcase off the

ground, then grins and says to James,
"Jolly good throwing James."
"Horse Shoe's Captain of the Boy Scouts."
Burke smiles and says, "A dead ringer you are at that. Let's
go." James picks up the soldier onto his back again and
asks him as everyone exits the storage room. "Since we've
met, I don't know your name."
"Jim is my name," replies Jim.
"Jim? I had no idea that…well…it's a pleasure
to meet you, Jim. I'm James."
"Likewise James."
Our friends continue their trek to the landing port.

  Back home on Earth, Debbie driving down the
road and looking at a piece of paper, decides to
pull over and look around her present location.
After observing the area, she looks forward and
pulls back onto the road in the direction of the
Taylor's Ranch.

  Davis driving through the City Streets at about
thirty miles an hour looks at a white mini van
exactly like James' driven by an elderly couple. As
he drives past them, his eyes suddenly widen as he
says, "Shit!" He whips his car around, tires screeching, then
burns the tires off into the direction of the Mini Van. He
speeds passed the Mini Van at about fifty five M.P.H.
scaring the hell out of the elderly couple, as they veer off
the road…horn
honking, and crash into a newspaper stand. One
of the papers lands on the windshield, and it reads:
Unidentified virus still growing!

Back above Silus in space, Zemious' ship remains

Unscathed, alone and the last of the Tre'toan ships posing a serious threat. On Zemious' Bridge, the Captain and crew now display a look of concern and worry as the Captain turns to Zemious, "My Lord, shouldn't we at least," Zemious interrupts fiercely, "No Captain! Again you question my authority! We will remain here...until I say otherwise!"
The Captain tips his head a little while looking at Zemious and says, "Once again My Lord...forgive me." The Captain turns to his console, and the entire crew watching the conversation, return to their duties as well.

Looking at a large entrance with a catwalk that leads upwards to the Silustrian Capital's landing port...our friend's walk through the entrance, and up the catwalk. Upon reaching the top of the catwalk, the sound of at least a thousand or more voices are heard cheering and celebrating the victory of the evil Tre'toan's failed attempt of annihilation. Our friends look in the direction of the landing area, and see a half dozen UFOs landing...and one already grounded, it being Burke's ship. His crew exits, waving with smiles. Deek and Burke wave to them. Burke then says to James, him still with Jim on his back,
"Whelp...I guess there's one more flight after all." James looking relieved and smiling replies, "And I'm looking forward to it, more than you know." Mirla walks over to the edge of the platform and begins waving her hands to the cheering crowd below. Suddenly four Silustrian men with a strange looking gurney that hovers, approach

James and Jim, stopping next to them with
smiles, and one of them says, "Take him we will,
help him now." James immediately helps Jim onto the
gurney, and Jim lying down says to James, "A true friend,
and brave you are." Jim smiles as James replies, "Thank
you Jim, and you take care, ok?"
James smiles as Jim adds, "Take care I
will, goodbye." James says, "Goodbye," as they take Jim
away. Burke, James and Deek join Mirla at the edge of the
landing platform, she still waving.
They stand next to her and look down to see
dozens of orbs flying all around, over the thousand
or more soldiers and citizens of Silus, cheering
and applauding in their celebration. Burke and
Deek wave to them, and James quickly holds his
hands up high, displaying peace signs.
The crowd cheering briefly increases. Burke and
Deek finishing waving, and Burke turns to James, and
James puts his hands down and looks
at Burke, while Burke then says, "Well...you'd better be
going now." James wears a curious look, as Burke hands
Deek the briefcase containing the serum.
"What are you saying Professor?"
Deek nods to Burke, and Burke nods back, as
Deek walks away. Burke continues,
"Don't worry James, Deek knows what to do...
and I assure you he'll take good care of you as
well." Mirla turns towards Burke and James...
thinking of what to say, or do upon James'
departure. "Why aren't you coming with us,"
asks James with a look of concern.
"My services are needed here...to be of
assistance in any further threat the Tre'toans may
have up their sleeves."

112

James smiles briefly then says, "I understand."
Burke wears a look of curiosity and asks,
"Tell me James…just what is your occupation
back home?"
James' eyes widen briefly as he sighs heavily and
tilts his head a little while replying,
"A News paper reporter…would you believe
that?" Burke still with a curious look asks,
"You don't say?"
James smiles and replies, "Don't worry
Professor, your secret's safe with me."
Burke grins and says, "I'd be more worried about
everyone's reactions back home, upon hearing such a
farfetched, and unbelievable story."
James chuckles and says, "Good point Professor."
Burke grins and says, "Yes."
Mirla wearing a smile walks up to James and briefly bows
to him and says, "I and the people of Silus, owe you our
complete gratitude. And we shall all miss you James
Lowery." She leans in, closes her eyes and kisses James on
the cheek. James remains smiling for the moment, as she
finishes kissing his cheek with
thankfulness.
"Thank you your majesty," says James as Burke
pulls out a Silustrian currency coin and hands it to
James. He takes it and Burke says, "Wouldn't
want you to go home empty handed now." James
nods and smiles, then extends his hand to Burke,
and they shake. "Thanks Professor."
"No…Thank you."

  Back home at the Taylor Ranch, James' Mini
Van is still parked where he left it, as Debbie
spots it and pulls up quickly, locks up the brakes,

and exit's her SUV quickly, running up to
James' van. She reaches it, looks in and sees the
digital scanner, then looks around the area in
front of the van and sees James' camera, and his
notepad and pencil on the ground. She picks them
up and looks at them for a moment…then with
tears running down her face, she looks up to the
stars that slowly become visible as the sun begins
to set.

Davis speeds down the highway, and finally
reaches the dirt portion of road, as a dust cloud
blocks the rear view of his car, disappearing from
sight.

Back at the landing platform on Silus, Burke and
Mirla wave goodbye, as Burke's ship begins to
take off. On the bridge of the ship, James stands at the
window and waves for a moment, then turns to
Deek and says, "Alright Deek, take me home,
safely." James sits down in the center of the bridge, and
straps himself in, as the rest of the five-crew
members assume their positions at their control
stations. Just above the atmosphere of Silus,
the ship approaches quickly, and zips by and
away.

Aboard Zemious' bridge, the Captain turns
quickly to Zemious and says with urgency,
"My Lord, our scanners have picked up a
Silustrian vessel approaching !"
"Lay in that course Captain, and pursue them
Now," demandingly says Zemious. Zemious' ship
suddenly zips away after Deek's.

114

Back aboard the bridge of the UFO, the deep pulsating alarms begin, as James looks at Deek and shouts, "What is it Deek?"
"Tre'toan ship fastly pursuing… a Command ship it is." James' eyes grow with fear, as one of the crew quickly runs to the gunnery station, now unfolding out of the ceiling. The crewman gets in it quickly and straps himself in…his hologram appearing, displaying Zemious' ship closing in. The blue containment beams suddenly kick in, as James says, "Round two, here we go."

  In space, Deek's ship zips by, as Zemious' ship fly's closely behind firing his huge laser cannons. Back aboard the UFO, the crewman at the gunnery aims ever so carefully and fires a direct hit to Zemious' ship, but does no damage. Wearing a worried look he says, "Uh oh." In space almost at light speed, the chase persists.

  Back on Earth on the now dark desert road, Davis still driving fastly suddenly sees a coyote in his headlights so he turns the wheel to avoid it and spins out into a ditch. "Oh hell! Not now!" Davis frustrated floors the gas, but only digs himself in deeper. "Come on," he shouts as he tries reverse, and digs himself in so deep, that he bottoms out. He slams his hands on the steering wheel, and shouts, "Damn Coyote!" He then uses his shoulder radio. "Nelson!" After a brief moment, Nelson responds, "Yes Sir?"

  At the Taylor's Ranch, Debbie sits in her SUV

looking at the stars through her rolled back
sunroof. "I know your somewhere out there James. And
I'm right here…waiting for you." She begins to
breakdown.

Back in deep space, the chase still in full swing,
with constant laser fire exchange.
Aboard the UFO, Deek touching several
lighted controls says to James,
"Hold tight Mr. Lowery, shortcut we will take!"
"Shortcut? What do you mean shortcut Deek,"
says James loudly, as he watches Deek nod
towards the bridge window. James quickly turns
his head toward the bridge window, and his eyes
widen with fear, as his jaw drops while looking at
a black hole getting closer. James slowly points at
it, then says, "D,d,d Deek? Is that a black hole?"
"No worry Mr. Lowery! Safe we will be!"
"Won't we be ripped apart,"
asks James as he begins to grip his chair ever so
tightly. Outside the UFO, a fluorescent blue
shielding system suddenly surrounds the entire
ship. Behind them, Zemious still pursues with massive laser
firing.

On the bridge of Zemious' ship, the crew still at
their posts, and Zemious still sitting in his chair
shouts, "Get us closer Captain!" The Captain replies, "My
Lord, they're attempting to enter the vortex just ahead of
our location!"
"They will not escape me!" The Captain looks at Zemious
with question and says, "My Lord…we can't," Zemious
quickly stands and his eyes glow with fire fiercely as he
says aloud, "You will Captain!"

116

After a brief moment, the Captain just turns
around to his console, then exchanges glances with
a couple of other crewmen...doubt in their eyes.

  Looking at the entrance to the black hole, the UFO dives
in quickly, and the front of the ship
begins to stretch. On the bridge, everyone, and everything
begins to slow down and stretch from the black hole's
effects. James tries to speak as his eyes, nose, and mouth
stretch forward about five inches. He slowly crosses his
huge eyes to look at his nose.

  Zemious' ship begins to enter the black hole, it
too stretching forward. On Zemious' bridge,
Zemious and crew also suffer the same effect, but
his ship begins to shake with tremendous
vibration. An alarm begins sounding. The crew
slowly falls to the floor, as the effects from the
black holes gravity are too unbearable.
Zemious screams "Noooooo!" As fire exits from
his eyes.

  Inside the black hole, Zemious' ship begins to
disintegrate and explode from the stern to aft.
After just a moment, he, his crew and the ship are
but granules of small debris.

  Looking downward at the UFO in the black hole, it holds
together well, as it is stretched to the shape of a cigar. On
the bridge, James still stretched rolls his big
eyes slowly to look at one of the crew, and the
crewman he looks at, his head and limbs
resemble that of a praying mantis with over sized eyes.

Somewhere in deep space closer to our galaxy, a
disruption followed by a spiraling of space matter
suddenly appears. Next, the UFO begins to exit.
On board, everyone still stretched, and seen through the
bridge window the end of the black hole appears. The
second they exit the end of it, everyone snaps back to
normal…the reaction is as if being punched.
James starts feeling his whole body and smiles
while saying, "I'm alive! I'm alive!"
He turns to Deek who doesn't look surprised at all
and asks, "How? How did we just manage that?"
Deek simply replies, "What is you call physics."
"That ship, where is it," asks James with
concern. "Destroyed it is." James wears a look of relief and
turns around towards the bridge window revealing light
speed travel. He points towards the bridge window and
says, "Onward mattes!"

Back home on the dark desert road leading to the
Taylor's Ranch, Davis leans back on his car with
arms crossed waiting for Nelson and Barnes to
arrive. Suddenly in the distance, headlights appear
coming up fastly towards Davis. After a moment,
the vehicle being the black SUV, pulls up behind
Davis's car and stops. Nelson and Barnes exit and
start walking towards Davis. Davis shoves off the
car, faces them while placing his hands on his
hips then says, "Well it's about damn time!"

At the Taylor Ranch, Debbie now asleep in her
SUV, and in her hands, she holds the picture of
her and James.

Just above Earth's atmosphere in space, Deek's

ship suddenly appears out of light speed, and flies
towards Earth. On the bridge, the crew still at the controls,
as Deek's blue containment beam shuts off and he walks
away from his station towards the entrance ramp that leads
to the lower portion of the ship. James looking at Earth
through the bridge
windows says, "We made it! I'm home!"
He then takes out the coin that Burke gave him and
stares at it while saying, "I won't forget you Professor."
Deek returns from the lower section, and walks to his
control console. James puts the coin away, and turns to
Deek, "So how does this serum,
evaporation thing work anyhow?"
"Hurry we must!" Deek ignoring his question as his blue
containment beam comes on and they suddenly fly in faster
towards Earth. Looking out the bridge
window, Earth's hot ozone layer appears and
disappears quickly, as James begins to grip his
chair again.

   Outside the ship, a clear misty steam begins to
exit the rear portion of the ship's very edge. The
ship suddenly begins to pick up more and more
speed, as it levels off at approximately three miles
above Earth.

   Inside the cockpit of an Airliner, a pilot and
copilot at the controls, when suddenly Deek's ship
zips right by them. They look at each other. "Did
you see something," asks the pilot.
"No. Must have been one of them experimental
planes." They both nod their heads.

   Back aboard the UFO, James with a frightened

look briefly shouts, "WOO." as the ship travels
thousands of miles per hour, dodging planes and
mountains the whole time.

On the ground at Max's gas and convenient
store, Tommy closing the store, finishes locking
the door, then turns and pulls out a pocket-radio
and places the earphones on, then turns on the
radio. He rocks out as he walks away from the
station. Suddenly Deek's ship streaks across the sky.
Tommy sees it and stops rocking out, as his eyes
fix themselves on the sky, and his jaw slowly
drops. Suddenly he sees it again, and pulls the
earphones off and stares at them!

On the dirt road to the Taylor's Ranch, Davis's
car now out of the ditch, and Nelson and Barnes
still there, as all three of them also watch the sky
as Deek's ship makes a pass every other second.
"What do ya suppose it is Chief," asks Nelson. Davis
replies, "Maybe them damn Tre'token creatures."

Aboard the UFO, James now laying low in his
seat grips it as hard as he can while squinting,
as the view through the bridge window is totally
obscure of any structure what so ever.

Six miles high above Earth looking down, the blue streak
from Deek's ship is seen, and getting faster by
the second, until it encircles the entire globe in a
matter of just eight seconds, then beginning to
slow down for four seconds until it's no longer
visible.

On board, James still squinting and gripping his
chair, opens one eye while saying, "Is it over yet?" Deek
replies, "Over it is." James eases back up in his seat and
opens his eyes, then release his chair and his hands remain
in a grip. "Earth, is it safe now Deek?" Deek replies, "Hope
so we do." Deek smiles.

   On the dirt road, Davis and his rookies watch in
the near distance, as Deek's ship heads for the
Taylor Ranch location. Davis shouts, "Come on,"
as he gets in his car, starts it up, and peels out
shooting rocks and dust all over Nelson and
Barnes, as they try to get in the black SUV.

   At the Taylor Ranch, Debbie still lays asleep in
the driver's seat, when suddenly her SUV begins
to shake, then rock back and forth. She wakes up
frightened, while all of the lights start flashing, horn
honking, and engine starting and stopping. She starts to
scream as the wind also gets heavy. Suddenly it
all stops, and out of nowhere about fifty yards
in front of her, the UFO starts to land. All the
animals begin to act spooked once again. Debbie's
eyes widen, and her mouth opens as she stays in
her SUV for the moment, just watching in
amazement at the incredible sight of the UFO
landing. After a moment, the UFO lands, and
bright lights suddenly shine on the ground from
it. Next, the access ramp begins to open
until fully extended to the ground. The animals
now begin to settle down. Debbie still with a frightened
look remains ever so still. Suddenly she sees a pair of feet
walking down the ramp, then legs, and finally the whole
figure of a man. Debbie decides

to slowly get out of her vehicle, not removing her eyes for
even a second, as she completes her daring exit, and stands
next to her vehicle, now with a look of
hope, as the man's dark figure clears the light
pollution. Debbie takes a step forward, then stops.
She sees James' face smiling, and she runs towards
him...finally reaching him and almost tackles him
as they embrace.
"Oh James, I thought I'd never see you again."
Debbie with tears of joy as James hugs her tightly
and says, "You know me sweetness...I can't stand
to be without you for a second." They quickly
lock lips for a moment...and while kissing, Debbie
opens her eyes and sees the crew carrying off the
Taylors on their shoulders. She unlocks lips
quickly while still staring at them. James turns
around while still holding her, and she curiously
asks, "What are they doing James?"
James grins and replies, "They...would be the
Silustrians. And what they're doing...is a long
story." Debbie looks at James, then back to the UFO and
sees Deek walking down the ramp, as the rest of
the crew returns to the ramp, walking back
into the UFO. Deek stops at the end of the ramp
and awaits James' farewell. James looks at
Debbie and says, "I've gotta go say goodbye to
my friend." Debbie just nods, as James turns her
loose and walks over to Deek. James starts the
farewell. "Well...I guess this is it Deek."
Deek nods once, as James continues,
"It was quite a ride, I can tell ya that."
"I thank you, James." Deek smiles and James
says, "And we thank you Deek, for believing in
the importance of peace and life...and answering

the call in a time when desperately needed."
Deek nods once again, then extends his hand.
James extends his hand and they shake hands.
"Take care Deek."
"Take care I will."
They finish shaking and James takes a couple of
steps back slowly, then turns and walks back to
Debbie. Halfway to her, he stops and turns around
to see Deek halfway up the ramp, facing him…as
Deek holds up a peace sign and smiles. James
smiles and holds up a peace sign, then Deek turns
and walks up into the UFO, and the access ramp
begins to close. James returns to Debbie's side
and they hold each other, watching the UFO
take off…as the wind once again blows
everywhere. The UFO about a hundred or so
feet off the ground begins to move away quickly,
and the wind stops. Debbie and James kiss heavily
once more. In the barn on the ground, the Taylors begin to
regain consciousness.

   On the road almost to the Taylor's, Davis driving
sees the UFO flying away. He floors the gas
even more.

   James and Debbie finally stop kissing, then turn
and start to walk back to their vehicles.
Davis suddenly arrives speeding up and stops,
gets out of his car quickly, and runs up to James
and Debbie. "We thought you was a goner. What did they
do to ya? Or take ya for that matter?"
James replies, "Chief, right now at this
moment…I've only got one thing on my mind."
James looks at Debbie and smiles. Davis takes a

deep breath and says, "All right you two…I
suppose you've been through enough already. Get
on outta here." James and Debbie still smiling at each
other, and James says, "There's some folks in the barn that
might need some attention Chief." Davis runs in the
direction of the barn as James and Debbie walk to their
vehicles. They walk over to Debbie's and
stop. Debbie suddenly turns to James with a look
of concern.
"There's an alien Virus James!" James calmly
replies, "Was a Virus. Hey, how'd you know
about it?" Debbie sighs and replies,
"It's a long story." James briefly displays
curiosity, then grins and says, "I'll drive."
"What about your Van?"
"It can wait." Debbie smiles and hands James the keys,
then runs around to the passenger side, and they both get in.
James starts it up, turns around, and pulls away. Nelson and
Barnes finally arrive and speed past James and Debbie.
James' voice asks,
"Honey…have we any fresh milk at home?"
"Why would you be thinking of milk at a time
like this?"
"Oh nothing…just curious."

  In space just above Earth, the UFO
approaches. On the UFO in the same quarters that James
first met Deek, lays James' boss, Olsen , restrained and only
in boxers. Deek enters and uses the cylindrical device to
wake him up.
In space looking at Deek's ship, Olsen's voice is
briefly heard screaming with fright, then Lila the
cow Moos, as the UFO zips out of sight.

THE END ?

ALIENS
BELIEVE TOO!

About the Author

Brian was born in Long Island N.Y by his
beloved mother Paulette .F Hiller, and late father
Robert N. Hiller Sr. His father being an aviation
machinist, developed and ran an Academy of
Aeronautical Machinery located in Long Island
N.Y. Brian's late grandfather Alfred Hiller, was
as well a pioneer in the early years as an
Aerospace Designer , also residing in Long
Island N.Y.

Like his father and grandfather before him,
Brian was also fascinated with the field of
aviation, and space exploration...yet in a different
perspective. All of his life, he's enjoyed writing
about his own thoughts and ideas about space
travel, and the endless boundaries of the
Universe, for the most part in fictional
characteristics. Brian also studied with other writers to
become more familiar with the entire conception, and
development of creating and writing unique, and
original literature. Brian being a screen writer as
well, looks forward to the opportunity of
someday directing movies of his own stories.

www.ingramcontent.com/pod-product-compliance
Lightning Source LLC
Chambersburg PA
CBHW031836170626
46807CB00004B/1493